T0199106

Dying to Celebrate

A Tourist Trap Mystery Bundle

Lynn Cahoon

LYRICAL UNDERGROUND
Kensington Publishing Corp.
www.kensingtonbooks.com

Books by Lynn Cahoon

The Farm-to-Fork Mysteries
Killer Comfort Food
Deep Fried Revenge
One Potato, Two Potato, Dead
Killer Green Tomatoes
Who Moved My Goat Cheese?

Novellas
A Pumpkin Spice Killing
Penned In
Have a Deadly New Year

The Tourist Trap Mysteries
Picture Perfect Frame
Murder in Waiting
Memories and Murder
Killer Party
Hospitality and Homicide
Tea Cups and Carnage
Murder on Wheels
Killer Run
Dressed to Kill
If the Shoe Kills
Mission to Murder
Guidebook to Murder

Novellas
A Very Mummy Holiday
Mother's Day Mayhem
Corned Beef and Casualties
Santa Puppy
A Deadly Brew
Rockets' Dead Glare

The Kitchen Witch Mysteries
One Poison Pie
Two Wicked Desserts

Novellas
Murder 101
Chili Cauldron Curse

The Cat Latimer Mysteries
A Field Guide to Homicide
Sconed to Death
Slay in Character
Of Murder and Men
Fatality by Firelight
A Story to Kill

LYRICAL UNDERGROUND BOOKS are published by
Kensington Publishing Corp.
119 West 40th Street
New York, NY 10018

All Kensington titles, imprints, and distributed lines are available at special quantity discounts for bulk purchases for sales promotion, premiums, fund-raising, educational, or institutional use.

Special book excerpts or customized printings can also be created to fit specific needs. For details, write or phone the office of the Kensington Sales Manager: Kensington Publishing Corp., 119 West 40th Street, New York, NY 10018. Attn. Sales Department. Phone: 1-800-221-2647.
Lyrical Underground and Lyrical Underground logo Reg. US Pat. & TM Off.

First Electronic Edition: March 2020
ISBN-13: 978-1-5161-0822-0 (ebook)
ISBN-10: 1-5161-0822-1 (ebook)

First Print Edition: March 2020
ISBN-13: 978-1-5161-0823-7
SBN-10: 1-5161-0823-X

Dear Reader,

One of the most frequent questions I get during Q&A is where did you get the idea for this book. It's funny how things happen in the publishing world. I was talking to my editor over dinner, telling her how excited I'd be about being in an anthology with some other cozy authors. It's a great marketing project where we all share our reader lists and, hopefully, we all get new readers. The conversation changed to a discussion of novellas in general and what I'd like to see in a Tourist Trap holiday novella. A few weeks later, I had an offer for three novellas. The plan was to release digital only first, then move to a print version later.

The hard part was we'd left Killer Party with a bit of a cliff hanger (Jackie dumping Harrold with no explanation) that would be resolved in Memories and Murder, the next full-length Tourist Trap book. I went to the past to find adventures for Jill and Greg. As a bonus, you'll see some of your favorite characters who have moved on to different lives.

Want the exact list?
GUIDEBOOK TO MURDER
MISSION TO MURDER
IF THE SHOE KILLS DRESSED TO KILL ROCKETS' DEAD GLARE (NOVELLA #1)
KILLER RUN
A DEADLY BREW (NOVELLA #2) SANTA PUPPY (NOVELLA #3)

Welcome back to South Cove. I hope you enjoy your stay.
—Lynn

Rockets' Dead Glare

A Tourist Trap Novella

Chapter 1

Power corrupts. Absolute power corrupts absolutely. Truer words were never spoken, especially in small towns where big fish rule. I think a lot about power and influence during our monthly South Cove Business-to-Business meeting. To be completely honest, sometimes I think about the cheesecake sitting in the walk-in cooler in my office, but mostly I think about relationships and secrets and small-town politics. Like today.

Bill Sullivan, our chairman and a city council member, had invited the volunteer South Cove fire chief to open up the meeting since there had been a few changes in policy approved by the council for the upcoming season. Unfortunately, Barry thought he'd been invited to lecture the group on the history of fire prevention, rather than just give a quick update of his program.

I'm Jill Gardner, and as the business liaison to the council I was responsible for hosting and setting up the meetings. By my count, today's group of business owners had gone through three rounds of coffee carafe refills and the cookie plates were totally empty. I shook my head when Sasha Smith, one of our baristas, asked me a nonverbal question about refills. We hadn't gotten our supply order from Pies on the Fly yet, and if the meeting didn't end soon, we'd be out of food to sell to actual paying customers.

"Safety is our number one priority." Barry Gleason stood in front of the shop owners gathered for the June meeting and pounded the table with his fist. The volunteer fire chief paused, and when he knew he had the crowd's attention, he ran a beefy hand with a garnet ring from his college football glory days through his wavy, too long salt-and-pepper hair.

Amy Newman, my BFF and the secretary for the meeting, leaned toward me and whispered, "Someone should tell him that hair style went away with the Bee Gees."

I tried to keep my lips from twitching, but from the glare I got from Mayor Baylor, I guess I had failed. I glanced down at the agenda. Once the fire chief relinquished his stage, the only other thing was Darla and the finishing touches for the Fourth of July street festival. Since the actual holiday was on a Saturday this year, we had a long weekend planned for South Cove visitors and tourists. Everyone would be open longer hours and Coffee, Books, and More would be erecting a tent annex out at the end of town near the bandstand and Diamond Lille's. Which the owner, Lille, had expressed her dismay about several times. Lille and I had an agreement mostly: she didn't come north and I didn't go south. Except for festival time when the needs of the tourists superseded our boundaries.

"I'll be inspecting each and every business this week for fire code violations. If you're not up to code, I'm going to close you down on June thirtieth until you are compliant." Barry started handing out folders. "These are the new rules. You all might have gotten away with being lax on the fire code before, but now with the city council's blessing, there's a new sheriff in town, so to speak."

"That's less than a week away," I said. I opened the folder and cringed when I found what looked like a twenty-five-page single-spaced list of must-do's. "It will take me that long to read and understand these regulations."

Barry shrugged. "Not my problem. You all didn't seem to worry about fire safety when I didn't have the power to make you change. Now you're on my timeline."

"I've always believed in following the rules," Josh Thomas, owner of Antiques by Thomas, said, jumping into the discussion. "You can come inspect my shop at any time. I'm certain I'll pass."

"Thank you for your support." Barry paused, looking for questions from the group who, like me, had their gaze on the enormous list of must-do's. To fill the gap in the discussion, Mayor Baylor started to stand, but Bill Sullivan beat him to the front of the table.

"Thank you, Barry, for that insightful update on the history of fire prevention in South Cove. Now, let's get this meeting going. I know you all have a lot to do before the holiday next week. Darla, would you come up and give us the final directions on the Fourth of July festival?" Bill moved in front of Barry, who still hadn't sat down.

Barry glanced at the mayor, who waved him into the seat next to him. Apparently, Barry hadn't been ready to relinquish the podium. He probably had planned on reading the entire list of regulations to us, one by one. Thank goodness for Bill. I don't say that often, but today he'd saved the entire group from dozing off at the table. Even with the excess of caffeine from the coffee.

Amy pushed a sheet of paper toward me. I picked it up and tried to read her scribbles. *Rumor is he has slept with all of his firefighter's wives.*

I picked up her pen and wrote in big block letters the only response I could muster: *EWWWW.*

Amy giggled and this time not only Mayor Baylor but Bill and Darla glared at me.

I squared my shoulders and mumbled, "I didn't do anything."

"If Jill will quiet down, I'll run through the assignments. Our big event will be on Saturday, when Diamond Lille's will host an old-fashioned summer picnic to go with our old-fashioned Fourth of July theme. We'll set up tables in the street with red-checked table cloths. And we have a great lineup of bands coming in all day. Matt did a great job of setting up a diverse mix." Darla blushed a bit as she threw kudos to her boyfriend-slash-winery manager. He'd arrived on the scene last winter and, like Sasha, hadn't left. That had been one of the mayor's great ideas that had actually worked out.

Well, except for the manager of the Welfare to Work program. But that's another story. I pretended to take notes as Darla listed off the events starting at noon on Thursday. All I knew was my store needed to be open and staffed until nine each night. Which were normal hours anyway. We would be down a person since Toby would be full-time deputy for the duration of the festival, but Amy had volunteered to take on a few shifts in the evening.

"You realize that these people you bring in for festivals are mainly drunks and losers." Barry was playing a game on his phone so he didn't see Darla's glare. But I did. She ignored his comment and went back to outlining the festival schedule.

As the meeting broke up, Barry Gleason barreled his way toward me.

"Since I had to stay for the entire meeting, I've already started the fire safety review for your shop. Do you mind if I check the back office? That way we'll be done and I can move on to Mr. Thomas's shop." Barry Gleason grinned and I realized that maybe this wouldn't be as bad as I'd imagined. He probably would take ten to fifteen minutes and I'd be done for the next year. "I'm sure you're as busy as I am," he said.

"That's for certain." I took his arm and led him toward the counter. "Sasha will assist you if you need access to anything or need information."

Sasha smiled brightly. "I'd be glad to help."

"Actually, I'd rather work with you, if you don't mind." Barry glanced at Sasha and even I could see the dismissal in his eyes. I didn't know if it was her age or her skin color that made him uneasy, but Barry had gone down a few pegs in my estimation of him—which hadn't been that high to begin with.

"That's fine. Sasha's busy with the counter anyway." I sent Sasha a "what can you do" glance and got a shrug from her back. Either Barry didn't like working with underlings or people younger than him, or, probably, he didn't want to work with anyone he didn't think was worth his precious time. Anyway, the faster I got him out of the shop, the better for all of us.

Ten minutes later, he ripped off a page that appeared to be a ticket. He'd been taking notes on the pad all through the tour, but I hadn't realized it was an official document. "Here's the list of infractions. Please call me when these are repaired and I'll come back for a new inspection. Call early as it typically takes a week to get on my schedule."

I glanced through the list. "For a lot of these things, I'll need to call in an electrician. There's no way I can get them done by June thirtieth. That's next week."

"Then you'll be closed until you do get them done. And I won't do any reinspections from July first to the seventh since it's a holiday week. I'm planning on taking some time off." He handed me a card. Then he winked. "Call me when you need a reinspection. Or if you think of a way we can work this out."

I dropped the list and the card on the counter. I wasn't quite sure what his idea of "working something out" was, but I didn't want to broach the subject here. And it wouldn't do to make a scene, but the mayor was going to get an earful as soon as I got him cornered. Glancing around the room, I realized I was too late to grab him after the meeting. The only people left were helping Sasha set the dining room back up. Which meant the mayor was long gone, since he didn't do manual labor.

Sasha glanced at me as she walked back to the counter. "Uh-oh. You look steamed. Did our esteemed fire chief insult you too?"

I held up the paper. "Actually, he gave me a list that is impossible to complete by the end of the week. Which means I'll have to be shut down over the fourth."

"That's not going to happen." Darla snapped up the list and read through it. "Most of these things aren't real violations. I think he made some of this up."

"Well, look out, he's on his way down the street and should hit the winery by midweek." I wondered if Amy had the skinny on what power this guy really had. Amy ran most of city hall and served as the mayor's go-to girl for whatever he needed. "I'm calling Amy to see if she'll have lunch with me."

"You could just call her and ask about the regulations," Darla said as she put a stack of flyers on the counter. "Hand these out to your customers. We need to get the word out about this festival. I want it to be the biggest one ever. The council spent enough on the entertainment, including bands and fireworks. I need to be able to show some ROI for their generosity."

When Darla left, Sasha picked up a flyer. "I know ROI is a business term, but what does it mean again?"

"Return on investment," Aunt Jackie said, answering the question from the back office. "Basically, the money or value you get from spending money. Like our advertisements that bring in people for the book signing. We spend $100 on ads, we get at least $100 in sales from the event. More if we have a good ROI."

My aunt was trying to teach someone the basics behind the business part of the store. She'd tried with me, but I really would rather be reading. Sasha was her next victim. One of these days I was going to feel sorry for my aunt and do something really stupid, like listen.

"I thought you'd be watching your shows." My aunt worked the late shift, but you never knew when she would pop down from the second-floor apartment over the coffee shop.

"I wanted to check in and see how the meeting went. Anything I need to know about?" Aunt Jackie poured herself a coffee as Sasha looked at me wide-eyed.

"How did she know?" Sasha whispered.

"She has the place bugged." I laughed as Sasha's eyes went even wider. "I'm kidding."

But there was a part of me that totally believed my aunt had a camera set up somewhere in the shop. I glanced upward toward the corners to see if I could see any flashing lights. When my gaze lowered, I realized my aunt was watching me.

"Okay, fine, there is a problem." I pushed the list of infractions toward her. "We're supposed to get all these done and have the place reinspected before June thirtieth. Or we'll be shut down."

"That's the only option?" my aunt said as she studied the list.

"Well . . ."

Now she looked up at me, her eyes narrowing. "Jill, what else did he say?"

"He insinuated that I could make it go away by calling him."

Aunt Jackie looked confused. "Why would calling him make these things go away? I'm not sure some of them are even possible to correct."

"I think he meant . . ." I glanced at Sasha, who was grinning.

"He wants Jill to be his love muffin," Sasha said, finishing my thought. "And can I say, EWWW!"

"That's what I said." I held my hand up for a high five.

My aunt watched us. When we were finished, she sipped her coffee. "This is a serious problem and I'd appreciate it if you treated it as such."

"I am." I sat next to her. "First thing, I'm reaching out to Amy to see what recourse we have on this whole thing. I can't believe the council gave him carte blanche to harass South Cove businesses. And then, if she doesn't know, I'm going to talk to Bill Sullivan. He should know what regulations the council put in place. And, if none of that fixes it, I have a few attorney contacts from my past career who would be happy to take on an overbearing fire department. We might even be able to get a cash settlement for pain and suffering."

"Which will mean our tax rate will increase. No one gets anything for nothing." My aunt shook her head. "Let me make a copy of this and I'll call an electrician to see what's really necessary and what's just this guy's opinion."

"Sounds like a plan." I waited for my aunt to disappear into the back office before I picked up my phone. "Hey, Amy, want to hit Diamond Lille's in about ten minutes?"

I listened to her tell me how hungry she was when I knew she'd eaten three cookies at the business-to-business meeting and probably had a three-egg omelet for breakfast. I would kill for her metabolism.

I'd already tucked my phone away when my aunt returned to the front. I took the copy she handed me and folded it into my tote. "Don't worry, we'll get this handled. No one's going to bully us."

"Government entities can do what they want in the name of safety for all. I would have thought you would have picked up on that by now." My aunt peered at Sasha. "Are you here by yourself this afternoon? Maybe I should come down and help."

"Toby's coming in at noon. There's no reason Sasha can't handle the shop by herself for thirty minutes," I said, stepping into the discussion before my aunt got Sasha to believe she wasn't trusted.

"Well, if you need me, I'm just watching television and working on an afghan. I like to get my Christmas gifts done early."

Sasha waited for Aunt Jackie to leave and didn't speak until we heard the door close at the top of the stairs. "Does she realize it's June?"

"I guess early is early." I grinned at my newest barista. "Be good or you'll get a knitted hat for Christmas instead of a bonus."

"I think a hat would be sweet." Sasha wiped the counter with a damp rag. "My granny is always making things like that for Olivia and me."

"You haven't seen Aunt Jackie's work yet." I tucked a new advanced reader copy of a local mystery author into my tote and then headed out the door. "I'll see you tomorrow."

By the time I power walked to Diamond Lille's, the place was already busy. Tuesdays seemed to be when the locals hit the diner, mostly to avoid the weekends full of tourists. Of course, a lot of locals worked weekends so eating out early in the week was more convenient. Amy had already snagged our favorite booth.

"What did you want to gossip about? Did you see Darla blush when she mentioned Matt. I can't believe she's still so crazy about him." Amy read over the menu as she talked, not looking at me at all.

Carrie dropped off our drinks. Iced tea with lemon. We've been going to Lille's for lunch for a while, so she knows what we want. We put in our orders and then I turned to Amy. "Tell me about Barry Gleason. What kind of regulation power did the council give him over the businesses?"

"I'm not exactly sure. I can pull up the minutes and send them to you. I don't really think they changed much last meeting. Maybe he's just exercising the power he already had. Why, was he harsh with the store?" Amy sipped her tea, watching me.

"Harsh is an understatement. He gave us so many citations that we'll never get them cleared in a week and he's threatening to shut us down over the holiday."

Amy's eyes widened. "No way. I'm sure that's not allowed."

"The problem is that he thinks it is. Get me the fire regulations so I have something to show him. I'm going to fight this guy tooth and nail." I sipped my tea and then groaned when Carrie dropped off my fish-and-chips basket. The smell of french fries makes me happy. I'm not proud of this fact, but it's the truth. I needed the salt, carbs, and fat today. Stress eating is my specialty. "I can't wait until he gives Josh his list of violations. I'm sure he'll go ballistic on him. Darla said that a lot of what he wrote me up for doesn't even make sense."

"Maybe he's got a brain tumor and doesn't know what he's doing." Amy took a big bite of her cheeseburger and wiped grease off her chin.

"Whatever it is, he needs to be reined in before someone thinks he's serious and does all this crap." I thought about Harrold, the older man who owned The Train Station. This kind of report on his shop could cause him to have a heart attack on the spot. "He's dangerous and needs to be stopped. I need to talk to the mayor."

"Uh-oh, I know that look in your eye. You're going to cause trouble." Amy pointed a french fry at me. "Maybe you should calm down first."

"Did I tell you what he said to me? How I could figure out some way to fix the issues if I met up with him? I don't think he was implying I could bribe him with *money*." I lowered my voice and glanced around the room. "It makes my skin crawl just thinking about him touching me."

"Wait, he wanted you to pay him off with carnal acts?" Amy almost choked on the french fry she'd just ate. "Man, that guy is creepy. He told Mayor Baylor that I was hitting on him last week. Barry had started to corner me in the hallway outside my office. I told him that if he came one step closer, I was going to punch him."

"What is it with some men? Does he think he's so attractive to women that we'll do whatever he wants?"

Amy took a sip of her tea. "I heard when his wife divorced him, she got alimony because she could prove he had been stepping out on her. I guess she had a good lawyer for the prenup and a premonition that he didn't know how to be faithful."

"Whatever he was, he's not going to push me or the other businesses in South Cove around like we're his chess pawns. I'm dealing with this now. Before Aunt Jackie calls in the lawyers." I broke off a piece of the battered fish. Tilting at windmills could wait until after lunch. I settled in to enjoy my food.

Chapter 2

"How did your day go?" Greg King, South Cove's police detective and my boyfriend, was sitting next to me in the swing on my back porch eating fried chicken straight from the bucket. I loved how he'd just show up with dinner and not expect me to cook all the time. Apparently, according to tonight's impromptu picnic, he didn't require me to set a table either.

"Besides finding out my store is a fire trap? Okay I guess. I had a good lunch." I glanced up from the chicken I was carefully pulling apart to share with Emma, my golden retriever. "Wait, you already knew, didn't you? That's why you brought dinner."

"I might have talked to Amy, who filled me in on your fight with our esteemed fire chief." He wiped his hands and face with a paper napkin. "Do you need a hug?"

"I need someone to rein this guy in." I fed the last piece of meat to Emma and tucked the rest of the food away in the box it came in. "Anyway, I don't want to talk about it."

"This must be serious if it's affecting your eating." Greg was able to dodge the biscuit I flung at him and Emma snapped it up.

"Let's talk about your work. Any hitches in preparing for the festival?" I put the box on the side table and gave Emma a shake of my head, warning her my leftovers weren't fair game. I love my dog, but sometimes she has a one-track mind. Especially when she smells fried chicken.

"We're bringing in some off-duty officers from Bakerstown for the weekend, but mostly it's business as usual. With a few thousand more visitors than a normal day." He gave the rest of his biscuit to Emma and stood to take his box out to the trash. "Toby told you he won't be able to cover any shifts that weekend, right? I've got him working full-time plus overtime this week. It's not that I don't trust the Bakerstown guys, but I know Toby and Tim."

"I get it. Toby's last scheduled barista shift was today. He's yours until the festival is over." I thought about the upcoming schedule. "Oh, and I'm working Aunt Jackie's shift tomorrow. She and Mary are going into town."

"Girls' night?"

"In a way. They both have doctor appointments in the morning, and then they're doing lunch and a shopping spree. She'll probably be home early evening, but I told her I'd take the shift. She's been working a lot lately. She needed the break." And, I thought, maybe she'd not be as grumpy if she got out of town for a while. My aunt was used to living in the city, where she could visit a museum or eat out at a fancy restaurant any night of the week. I loved having her here, but South Cove ran at a slower pace than she was used to.

"No worries. I've got a final planning meeting for the festival with Darla and the council tomorrow anyway." Greg and I were only dating, but it felt like more. Probably because we saw each other at least once a day. He lived in an apartment outside of town, but he liked hanging at my house more. And he loved Emma. All in all, it wasn't a bad situation.

* * * *

The next morning, I called Amy to see if she had found the regulations. Her tone told me that the mayor was standing over her and she couldn't talk. But I did get a promise to have a return call by the end of the day. The shop was empty after my commuter crowd had wandered in for morning java on their way to work. Aunt Jackie had talked to an electrical contractor who was coming in on Thursday for a look. I glanced at the list of "violations" and did the simple ones like unpacking the few boxes of books I'd stored by the back door. I even got on chairs and cleaned the dust off the ventilation covers. By the time Sasha came in for her shift, the place was gleaming, the bookshelves were all stocked, and I was beat.

"The place looks amazing." Sasha grinned. "Slow morning?"

"That and too much energy from being anxious about this whole Barry issue. I swear, I'd like to tie him to a chair and shave off that long hair he's so proud of. He looks like he's lost in the seventies." I sank on a stool, sipping the mocha I'd just made for myself. "But at least I can say we're making progress on the issues."

"I heard Josh Thomas got a three-page list. Kyle says he thought Josh was going to have a stroke right there and then." Sasha got settled behind the counter, washing up and putting on an apron before pouring her own coffee and joining Jill.

"You and Kyle talk a lot." I hid my grin behind my cup and took a sip. Sasha shrugged. "He's becoming a friend. He really likes working for Mr. Thomas. Although, at first, he thought his boss had a stick up his butt."

"The kid's a good judge of character." I personally *knew* Josh actually *had* a stick up his own butt, but I let that slide. Are the two of you serious?"

Sasha choked on the sip of coffee she'd just taken. "What, like dating? No way. He's not my type at all. I go for a more alpha guy. Someone who knows what he wants."

"You've been reading too many romances." I smiled at the reference to the popular hero type in the romance genre.

"I did want to talk to you about someone though . . ."

Darla burst into the shop before Sasha could finish. "I swear, I'm going to kill that guy."

I glanced at Sasha, who read my unspoken request and stepped around the counter to make Darla's favorite drink, a double-shot mocha, extra whip. "I'd ask who, but I'm pretty sure I know. I take it Wild Fire Barry made his way to the winery."

"Not only the winery, but every business from midtown up to my place. They all have a list of violations and a threat from him to close them until after the festival at best. I've been handling calls all morning." She grabbed the cup from Sasha and took a long sip. "Thanks, but give me another in a to-go cup. I'm heading over to camp out at the mayor's office today until he calls off his dog and fixes this problem."

"He can't close the entire town, can he?" Sasha set the to-go cup on the counter and came back around to sit with the group.

Darla snorted. "He can try. And he's making my life hell right now with all the phone calls I'm getting. Luckily, I already knew what he'd done to you, so I had some background when the calls started last night. Otherwise, I would have gone ballistic."

"Well, I've done all the corrections I can, and we have an electrician coming in tomorrow for a review of the rest, but I'm thinking he'll clear most of these as nonissues." I'd had the place gone over and any old wiring replaced before I'd opened the shop six years ago. Especially since I was going to live in the apartment above the store. Now that my aunt lived there, I was grateful I'd spent the extra time and money on bringing the place up to code. "I'll let you know what I find out, but Amy's trying to pull the city regulations and see exactly what power this guy has over South Cove."

"I don't care what the regulations are. He's not ruining my festival." Darla slid off the stool she'd just climbed onto. To say Darla was short was an understatement. The woman couldn't have been over five foot. But what she lacked in height, she made up in determination.

I felt better somehow knowing Darla was championing the cause. Maybe the mayor would listen to her. My history with the mayor was more of a hate relationship than a love-hate one. And we both liked it that way.

"Of course, Matt says I'm overreacting. He says Barry's a pretty good guy, just a little intense. But he *has* to say good things about Barry. Matt's still trying to get approved as a full-time volunteer for the crew." Darla shrugged. "Did you know they get paid for every call out? He wants the money so he can save for his own place. He says we're moving inland and starting a farm as soon as we can swing it. Can you see me as a farmer's wife?"

Laughing at the idea, Darla made her way out of the bookstore. I glanced at the clock. "I better get going as well. If you need help, call Nick first; he's looking for some more hours. If he's not around, I'll come in early." Nick Michaels was our summer barista who tried to work as many hours as he could. This job was his only source of cash since his mom didn't want him working during the school year.

"Sounds good. But I'm sure I'll be fine. Yesterday was pretty slow." Sasha turned toward the coffee bar and started wiping it down. I headed home to grab some lunch and settle in with the mystery I'd started last night. The best thing about owning a bookstore is reading the new releases. The second-best thing? Drinking great coffee while you're doing it.

* * * *

"Hey, beautiful." Greg walked into Coffee, Books, and More the next morning just after eleven. The morning had been busy, with the homeschooling group coming in for their monthly bookstore visit. I was always so impressed by the books the kids ordered and read. They all seemed to be reading above their grade level. But then again, I didn't know much about what kids should be reading. Sasha came in early to help with the group and I managed the coffee bar while they were there.

"Hey, yourself." I glanced at Sasha, who nodded and headed back behind the register. The majority of families had already left, with just a few stragglers who couldn't make up their mind between books. I stepped around the counter and gave him a hug. "I missed you last night."

"Sure you did. I bet as soon as you got home you heated up some pizza rolls and sat on the couch reading." He gave me a quick hug and I could smell the soap he typically used.

Greg knew me too well. Maybe I was going to have to up my game with him. Or I could just let him actually know the real me. I figured that was the road of least resistance. "Guilty as charged. Did you just come over to give me grief about my snacking habits?"

"I came to see if you'd have lunch with me over at Diamond Lille's. Next week's going to be crazy busy with the festival and we won't have time to just sit and talk." He smiled and brushed a stray hair out of my face. "I like just sitting and talking, among other things."

"If I get to keep the store open." I glanced around the shop. "Aunt Jackie's electrician is coming at five to check things out."

"You may not need to do much. I overheard Darla and the mayor going at it yesterday. She's hot under the collar, but she has good points. I think Barry has gone over the edge with his inspections. He even made a list of violations at the police station." Greg looked a bit uncomfortable. "I told him he could take them up with the mayor, but there was no way I was going to close down the station."

"He seems like he thinks it's his way or no way." I glanced at Sasha. "Let me grab my purse from the back and I'll be ready."

"Hurry up, woman, I'm starving," he called after me.

As I passed by Sasha, I winked. "Men. They all think they are in charge."

"You two are so cute together. And Greg is so totally alpha." Sasha rang up ten books the last homeschooling family had stacked on the counter. The kid who'd held everyone up had gotten both books, probably since he couldn't decide. Either way, it was a great ploy to get a second book out of a busy mom. The kid had style.

I grabbed my purse and as I headed back out to the front, I saw Greg on the phone. He cut it off when I walked up. "Don't tell me, you got called back in."

"Maybe. There's a problem down at the end of Beal Street. I guess there's a controlled burn out there by that old barn. But they can't find Barry." Greg glanced at me. "You want to take a short ride with me before lunch?"

"Sure, I have a book in my purse in case you're delayed." Besides, it would be a great chance to actually talk to Barry. "I think that would be an excellent idea."

Greg took my arm and led me to his truck. He opened the side door for me and then crossed over to the driver's side. Starting the engine, he looked at me. "You have to promise you won't cause a scene when we locate Barry."

"Why would I do that?" I tried to look noncommittal.

Greg pulled the truck out into traffic. Or out into the no traffic. I liked slow days in South Cove. It made the rest of the time bearable. As he drove out of town, Greg turned up the music and smiled at me. I liked that about us. We didn't have to talk all the time. We liked spending time together. A lot of evenings we sat on the couch and, while he watched whatever game was on, I would read. Emma would lay at the end of the couch sleeping. It felt right.

I leaned forward as we got closer. The flames were gone, but the building wasn't totally demolished. It was like they'd turned on the hoses to put out the fire a few minutes too early. "Whose property is this?"

"Barry's. He got it from his parents when they passed. I've heard rumors that he was planning on selling off to a condo developer. I guess that was one reason our mayor loved the guy so much." Greg pulled the truck up next to an ambulance. His brow furrowed and he glanced over. "Maybe they found Barry."

South Cove had three emergency vehicles—two fire trucks and an ambulance—beside the two patrol cars Greg's deputies used. And they were *all* parked on the edge of the road. We climbed out of the truck.

Greg shot a glance back at me. "You may want to stay here, just in case."

"Whatever." I shook my head and followed him into the crowd. I may not be able to cross the police barrier, but I wasn't waiting in the truck like a good girl. I paused next to Bill, who was covered with ash and water. His face was black from the soot.

He glanced at me and then scanned the area until he saw Greg. "Finally," he muttered.

"What happened?" I asked Bill as Greg walked up to Toby, who was flanked by the EMTs.

"We had a practice burn this morning. I figured Barry just wanted to get this property cleared and if he called it a training exercise, the city would pay for the removal and cleanup." He cleared his throat. "This is his place."

"Yeah, Greg told me that." I was watching the men gathered around the front of the partially burned building. "But what happened? Why is the ambulance here?"

"Barry set up the fire, and then he just disappeared. We thought it was because he wanted us to problem solve as a team. By the time we realized he was trapped in the building, it was too late." Bill ran his fingers through his graying hair. "I can't believe I'm still volunteering after all these years. Maybe Mary is right and I need to hang up my fireman's hat."

"I'm sure you do a great job," I started to say. Then Bill's words hit me. I glanced over at the group standing outside the charcoaled building and my stomach flipped as I realized why they weren't going inside. I knew the answer before I even asked the question. "Barry was in the house?"

"Barn, but yeah. He got caught in the fire." Bill must have seen my arm shaking because he grabbed hold and steadied me. "I'm sorry, Jill. Barry's dead."

Chapter 3

Greg tucked me into Toby's car and sent me back to town with my barista. Toby needed to be available for emergencies and I just needed to get out of there. I hadn't liked Barry one bit, but to die like that? It made me queasy. Once I got home, I curled up on the couch and turned on the television for the next several hours. I wasn't surprised to see my aunt walk through the door at about eight with a couple of takeout bags from Diamond Lille's.

Emma sat at attention to greet Aunt Jackie. It was almost like the dog knew she was fragile. Aunt Jackie ignored her and narrowed her eyes at me instead. "I figured you'd be here wallowing. No use crying over Barry. The man was worthless."

"I wasn't crying over him." I pulled the afghan closer, shuddering at the memory. "It's just a horrible way to die. You should have seen that building."

"Mary sent me pictures. I guess Bill took some shots before he left. He's pretty torn up too. Mary said he hated Barry, but I guess Bill feels guilty or something." My aunt nodded toward the kitchen. "Come help me set up dinner. I'm starving."

"I'm not sure I can eat." My aunt was right. Barry wasn't anything to me, but still, I felt affected by his death. Not sad, but shocked. I followed her into the kitchen and slumped into a chair at the table.

My aunt continued to unpack the bags like she hadn't heard me. "Lille says she's going to be watching our booth at the festival to make sure we don't overstep our boundaries. No chips, no food—just desserts, coffee drinks, and the normal things we sell out of the store."

"What does she think, we're going to start flipping burgers and selling hotdogs in a booth?" I pulled one of the containers toward me and opened it. A grilled ham and cheese sandwich, heavy on the ham, with melted provolone on the sourdough bread. And I knew there would be Dijon mustard smeared on the bread. I picked up the offering and took a bite. Heavenly. I wiped my mouth. "That woman needs to get a life. She's so busy making sure no one is getting one over on her she can't have any time or brainpower to have any fun."

My aunt let me rant until the sandwich was finished. Then she smiled and got up to pour herself another cup of coffee. "There, you look better with some color in your cheeks."

I glanced at the empty container. I'd even eaten the dill pickle spear. But to be fair, Lille's did have quality pickles. "You got me off track so I'd eat."

"I rarely had to do that when you were a child, but the technique still works." She pushed around her tuna salad on tomato with a fork. She ate like a bird. I, on the other hand, ate like a grown woman. Or a rhino. It didn't matter. Tomorrow Emma and I would go for a run on the beach and burn off the calories.

"Thanks for coming over." I got up and made myself a cup of herbal tea. I had to be awake at the crack of dawn tomorrow for my shift. No way was I ingesting more caffeine. I'd never sleep. "So how was your day with Mary?"

My aunt smiled and told me all about their trip to the city. Where they went, what they ate, who they saw. Then she paused, her eyes wide open. "Oh my, I almost forgot."

I dunked my tea bag into my cup a few times, stifling a yawn. "Forgot what?"

"I saw that man at the doctor's office. Well, not my doctor's office, but in the lobby. He was coming out of the elevator as Mary and I were getting in. He walked right past us and didn't say a word. Mary thinks he's a little deaf. I just blame it on a total lack of manners. Some people were just raised by wolves."

I stretched, knowing I was going to crash soon, but it didn't do any good to try to hurry along my aunt's stories. They had their own pacing. "So who did you see?"

"That man, you know, the one who died?" Her eyes narrowed. "I wonder why Barry Gleason was visiting a doctor on the day before he died."

We chatted a little longer, mostly about Mary and Bill and how he had no business doing something that strenuous. As I thought about the volunteer team we had, I realized a lot of the members were in their late forties. There weren't a lot of people who wanted to, or could, give up that much time to train and be on call. Toby and Tim both wanted to serve, but with their duties as police deputies, they didn't have time. As it was, I was constantly switching up Toby's schedule to accommodate his other jobs' hours.

Finally, my aunt gave in and cleared up the kitchen. She bagged the containers, and grabbing the trash bag, she gave me a quick hug. "Go to bed. You look like you haven't slept in a week."

"Well, between this and worrying about the shop, I've been a little upset." I stood to walk her to the door. "Thanks for bringing dinner."

"I wanted to check on you anyway." My aunt was heading out the door. "Roger left me a list of the things that do need to be corrected. I guess the electrician you used a few years ago had some shoddy work habits."

"Wait, what? Barry was right?" I sagged against the doorframe. My aunt had paused in the driveway to drop the trash off into the garbage can. "How much is that going to cost?"

"We'll talk about it tomorrow. Roger laughed at a few of the items and crossed them off our list. The ones that weren't code violations, that is." My aunt climbed into her tiny sedan and pulled out of the driveway.

"Get some sleep, she says." I shut the door and aimed my words to Emma. "Then she tells me we need major electrical work done. How am I supposed to sleep after hearing that?"

Emma woofed, which could have meant *Poor Jill.* But I'm pretty sure it was actually *Can you let me out?* I started shutting off lights and headed to the kitchen to wait for my dog so we could go to bed. Barry Gleason wouldn't be there to close our store down, but I still felt a responsibility to fix the items that Aunt Jackie's Roger had found in his inspection.

* * * *

Greg showed up at the coffee shop as I was getting off for the second day in a row. "Hey, do you want to try for lunch again? I'm waiting for Doc Ames's report on the autopsy and I'm holding off on a more in-depth interview of the guys from the training crew until I at least get Doc's take, so I'm at a standstill." He glanced at the empty coffee bar. "Or are you stuck here?"

"Nope, Sasha's in the back opening the book order that came in yesterday. I can go anytime. Just let me tell her she's on her own." I went into the back office and grabbed my purse. "Sasha, I'm out of here. You going to be okay?"

The girl looked like she was lost in thought, staring at a stack of new paperbacks she'd piled on the desk. "What?"

"I'm going to lunch with Greg. Do you need me to stay for a bit?" I considered her reaction and smiled. Maybe this thing with Kyle was more serious than she'd wanted to admit. It appeared my barista was in love.

"No, I'll come out. Let me grab this last pile of books." Her breath caught as she hurried to get out front. "Have fun at lunch."

"If you need help, call Aunt Jackie. She'll come in early." I followed her out to the main dining room and headed to Greg who was looking at a sports book. "I can get you a good discount on that if you're interested."

He sat the book down and took my arm. "I should get a *great* discount since I'm dating the owner of the place."

"I hear she's not so generous with her boy toys." I turned and waved at Sasha. "See you tomorrow."

We were just a few feet down the street when Greg spoke again. "The girl looks distracted. Something going on?"

He's got cop's eyes. The man saw everything. I put my arm in his and leaned close. "I think she's in love."

"Who's the lucky fellow?" Greg walked me across the street and into Diamond Lille's.

The smell of fried food layered with cheesy pasta and sweet desserts all mixed together almost knocked me over. I wouldn't want Lille to know this, but I loved this place. That's one of the reasons I stayed on her good side. The dishes that came out of Tiny's kitchen made me happy. And I liked being happy, especially around food. Suddenly, I remembered that Lille's cook Tiny was another member of South Cove's volunteer fire fighting crew. I cast a side-eyed look at Greg as Lille led us to a booth near the back.

When we were sitting with iced teas in front of us and our orders taken by Carrie, my favorite waitress, I leaned closer. "Did you plan this?"

"To have lunch with you? Yes, I did plan it. Remember, we were going to yesterday, but the whole date thing got a little messy." He put his hand on mine. "You never said who Sasha was lusting after."

"I never said lusting." I didn't move from my perch over the table. I didn't want anyone hearing my question besides Greg. "No, I meant, did you plan to come here because Tiny was part of the training burn yesterday? Is he a suspect?"

"No more than Bill or any other of the guys. Look, I just want to have a quiet meal where we don't talk about murder or suspects or clues." He squeezed my hand. "What do you say, can we try to appear normal for an hour?"

"Sorry, I just got carried away." Now I leaned back and slipped my hand out from under his. I took a long sip of my drink and tried to think of a subject that wouldn't lead us back to his job or mine, for that matter. "Oh, yeah, Sasha. I'm not totally sure, but she did mention Kyle."

Greg stirred sugar into his tea. "Well, I hope that's not true because I know Kyle has a girlfriend in Bakerstown. I ran into them there one day when I had to testify at the courthouse. She works there in the prosecutor's office. I think she might be prelaw."

"I don't believe it. Kyle, South Cove's version of the tattooed man, has a girlfriend in a justice career? What do they talk about?" When the kid first showed up for his volunteer gig with Antiques by Thomas, he'd had so many visible piercings he probably set off all the alarms at the airport just by walking through the front door. "I guess it's good to have close connections in the legal field."

"You date a cop. What do *we* talk about?" Greg must have anticipated the answer because he held up his hand. "Don't even go there. Besides, our food is coming."

Carrie dropped off our lunches. "Have you . . ." A crash in the kitchen interrupted her thought. As she turned toward the sound and headed out of the dining room, she said, "Sorry, enjoy."

"Aunt Jackie brought over food last night after her shift. She thought I was all upset over being at the scene of the fire yesterday. Am I that easy that all I need is food to make me feel better?" When Greg didn't answer, I looked up from arranging my french fries. "What?"

"Discretion is the better part of valor. Or something like that. Who said that anyway?" This time it was me who didn't respond. "Seriously, I'm not even touching that comment. How's your aunt doing? She seems to have settled into life here in South Cove easy enough. That must have been a hard transition, coming from the city."

"She seems okay. I think sometimes it's difficult because of all she left behind. But she has Mary here and they seem to do a lot together." I dipped a fry into Lille's special sauce, which looked a lot like her Thousand Island dressing. "And the quote is from Shakespeare. Sometimes your knowledge of literature surprises me, Mr. King."

"I don't just read the sports page, darling." He took a bite of his burger and groaned. "And to broach your other question, there isn't anything wrong with finding pleasure in food when it's this good."

That's why we got along so well. He got me. I cut my own burger into two halves and took a bite. "Oh, she did say one thing that was strange. And before you go all 'stop investigating' on me, I didn't ask her to tell me this."

Greg sat his hamburger down. "Am I going to even want to know?"

"I think so. Although I can't imagine how it would be important to your case." I glanced toward the kitchen where I could just see Tiny's head through the warming station. "I still don't think any of the men on your short list could have killed Barry. I was mad enough at him to spit nails, but killing him? Yeah, that's a whole 'nother level of angry."

"So what did your aunt say?" Greg's question brought me out of my mental wanderings.

"Oh, yeah. She said she ran into Barry at the doctor's office. Well, not at *her* doctor, but in the lobby of the building. The whole building is different medical providers. She sees both her primary doctor there and her rheumatologist." I could see by Greg's look that he thought I was getting off point again. "Look, that's all I know. She and Mary were getting in an elevator and Barry came busting out. Aunt Jackie said she called to him, but he didn't answer. Mary thinks he's deaf."

A twist of a smile curved Greg's lips. "Mary always sees the good in people."

His phone beeped and he pulled it out to read the text. I could see that the news wasn't good.

"Crap. I need to run to Bakerstown and see Doc Ames. The autopsy results are in." He pushed away his half-eaten burger as he put his phone back in his pocket.

"You should finish eating. I know how you get on investigations; you don't take time for yourself at all. Besides, it seems like a simple report. Barry died in the fire." I shivered, thinking about how painful that must have been. "Why can't he just fax it over?"

Greg took cash out of his wallet and set it on the table. Then he stood, kissing me on the top of the head. "Because Barry was already dead when the fire was started. This wasn't an accident. I'll call you when I have a chance."

I watched as he walked out of the restaurant. And then I realized, someone else was also watching Greg leave. Tiny, the cook, stood at the doorway to the kitchen, his face showing no emotion as he watched Greg. Then he glanced my way and flushed. Before I could figure out what that all meant, he disappeared back into the kitchen.

I grabbed my notebook out of my tote and, as I finished my lunch and a few of Greg's fries, I made notes about what I knew about Barry Gleason. I'd already talked to Bill, who had to be on Greg's list of suspects, but wouldn't be for long. Tiny, one of the other fire fighters who was there that day, was working and there was no way Lille would let me go back into the kitchen. So that left one person I could talk to about Barry's death. And as long as Darla wasn't there to protect him, I should be able to find him at the winery. Matt Randall was new to our little town, as he'd arrived as part of our internship program last winter. Not saying it was always the new guy who was guilty, but I wondered what he might have to say about the training incident gone wrong.

I finished my meal and tucked my notes back into my tote. I could walk to the winery, talk to Matt, and then be back at the house by two to let Emma out. I really needed to think about getting a dog door for her, but I wasn't sure about having her loose in the backyard without me there.

Instead of heading to the winery, though, I turned west and headed to the house. I'd let Emma out, then come back to talk to Matt. The plan set, I walked home, enjoying the midday sunshine as I thought about anyone else who could have wanted Barry dead. The problem with that line of thinking was, I'd have to include everyone in town who he'd "inspected" over the last couple of weeks. I'd wanted to kill him but I knew I didn't act on that instinct. What if someone with a business he'd threatened did?

But then I went back to the scene of the crime. There were only four people there when Barry died. Barry, Bill, Tiny, and Matt. I was pretty sure Bill hadn't reacted to a threat to South Cove Bed and Breakfast. He could have just changed the council's grant of power to the fire chief. Besides, Bill wasn't the killer type. Which left Tiny and Matt top on my suspect list.

Chapter 4

I'd let Emma out to do her business, grabbed a bottle of water for the walk, and was on my way back to town when I was sidelined by my neighbor. Esmeralda waved me down and quickly crossed the street. She wore her other uniform, a fortune-teller outfit, so I assumed she had reading appointments scheduled for the day. During the week, Esmeralda was South Cove's police dispatcher, so if I didn't run into her at home, I usually saw her at the police station when I visited Greg.

"Jill, I'm so glad I caught you this morning."

I didn't point out it was already after noon; instead, I smiled and nodded. "I'm actually on my way back into town."

"I figured you'd be snooping around today. Too bad about that poor man. He was a flirt every time he came into the station. Definitely not my type, too pushy and controlling. I like my men more pliable but it didn't stop him from trying to take me out." Esmeralda glanced down the street. My gaze followed but I didn't see anything.

"You have clients coming?" I wasn't sure if "client" was exactly the term to use for people who paid Esmeralda to do her mumbo-jumbo stuff, but I did know that people came on a regular basis. The woman was busy, for someone who had set up shop in a small town out in the middle of nowhere. South Cove got a lot of tourist traffic, but Esmeralda would have had a lot more repeat customers if she lived closer to the city. Her driveway was full most weekends with people who wanted to either talk to the dead or learn their future. Looking forward, looking back—people really just needed to enjoy the present.

"I know you're not a believer, but I appreciate your trying to make conversation. You're a good neighbor." Esmeralda pushed a strand of curly hair out of her face. "Anyway, I had a dream about you last night and I wanted to let you know."

"You're dreaming of me?" I wasn't sure what to say. "That's nice?"

"Not that way. My dreams are more prophetic than emotional. Although you are very lovely, I play for the other team." Esmeralda laughed at her joke. "Anyway, the dream was a bit fuzzy, but I did get one clear message out of the spirits. You'll never find what you're looking for until you look for something else."

My aunt had used that technique for years to find her keys. It was good advice, even if it came from the other side. "So I should stop looking for something?"

"Exactly." Esmeralda grinned and nodded to her house. "Sorry, I need to get inside before they arrive. It's kind of a staging thing for the whole experience."

"I don't see anyone coming." I glanced back down the street. Empty. Which is another reason I loved living in South Cove. On nonweekend days, our traffic was slim to none.

Esmeralda was already halfway across the street when she said to me, "I do."

I watched her disappear into her house. The woman was unusual. That was certain. Okay, so I could go with weird and still be on point. But she was a good neighbor and she'd watched Emma one weekend when Greg and I went out of town. So she had a few little oddities that you had to accept. I started up the hill toward town and that's when I heard the car engine.

Turning back, I saw a Land Rover turn off the highway and up Main Street. It pulled into Esmeralda's driveway, and as I watched, an older woman climbed out of the driver's side. Her gray hair was cut short and her casual linen pantsuit flowed in the breeze. Esmeralda had to have known what time the woman would arrive. There was no way she could have either seen or heard the car when she cut short our talk and returned to her house.

I headed back to town, thinking of Esmeralda and her gift and the idea of not looking for what I was trying to find.

By the time I got to the winery, I was hot and annoyed. Esmeralda's dream had made me grumpy. I decided I didn't want the spirits, or anyone, telling me what to do. I walked into the large barn that held the tasting room and the winery. Darla had the space to add on a dining area, but besides the small snacks she kept behind the bar, she claimed she had no desire to change South Cove Winery into a drinking and eating establishment.

The light inside the bar was dim, but I could see Matt working at the stage at the end of the room, setting up equipment for this weekend's musical guest. He'd brought in several bands the last six months that had increased the winery's draw of customers. Darla had put him in charge of the festival's entertainment too. Matt knew his music. I ordered a beer off their grocery store bottle list from the woman setting up the bar for the evening, and once I'd paid her, I took my bottle over to the stage.

"Hey, Jill, what are you doing out this early?" Matt grinned at me. "I figured you'd be working still."

"I'm the morning slave. After noon, I'm free to do anything." I glanced around the room. "I guess you and Darla are night owls around here."

"Yeah, we don't get a lot of day customers. But sometimes we get a bus full of tourists who want the winery experience." He flipped out a cord and started winding it up. "I'm trying to get this mess cleaned up. Barry gave Darla a hassle about how much equipment we have plugged in over in this corner. I think I can get a few things moved, but realistically, you need a lot of power for the bands' equipment."

"Of course, Barry's not around anymore." I watched his reaction to see what kind of emotion I'd get.

He sank down on the edge of the stage. "Yeah, I know. But he was right about the wiring. I guess I'd like to honor him by at least getting this corrected."

I saw sadness cross his face. I tried to keep the surprise out of my response. "You liked Barry?"

Matt nodded, looking down at the wires in his hands. "Barry was a tough nut to crack, but he took a chance on me and let me into the fire fighter group. He didn't have to, not with my past."

I didn't know much about Matt's past, except for the fact he'd been assigned to the work program last winter. I sat next to him on the edge of the stage and took a sip of my beer before I asked, "What do you mean?"

He glanced around the now-empty room. Even the bartender who had helped me was in the back, probably getting more product to stock for the evening customers. "Hell, I guess it doesn't matter now. I'm sure the new chief won't be as forgiving as Barry was, at least with me." He turned toward me. "But I'd appreciate it if you kept it between us."

"Darla is my . . ."

He cut me off before I could finish my sentence. "Darla knows everything. Do you think I'd even start a relationship with her if I wasn't going to be completely honest?"

"No, I guess not." The fact was, I didn't know Matt very well, and I had worried about what his intentions were with my friend. Darla had a big heart and a quick wit that kept everyone around her happy. She deserved a great guy. But I was willing to withhold judgment until I heard Matt's story.

"I got out of prison last year."

My eyes must have shown my shock because he laughed.

"Before you run away screaming, let me tell you the situation. I was a troubled kid. Never wanted to be in school, always wanted the fast money, cars, and girls." He smiled at the memory. "When I dropped out, I started hanging with some friends. Well, actually, they were a gang and had a nice business in stealing cars and selling them to a chop shop. I didn't even complete my first assignment before I was arrested. I guess I'm a horrible thief."

"You were in a gang, stole a car, and went to prison?" Matt didn't look that old. "What were you, sixteen?"

"Nope, just two days after my eighteenth birthday. I was tried as an adult. My folks had washed their hands of me years before so I didn't even try to ask for help." He shrugged. "I did my time and realized when I was in there that my so-called friends never visited or helped me out while I was inside."

"You find out who are your real friends when you really need them." I guessed that was a truism no matter what type of trials you were going through.

"For sure. So when I got out, my probation officer approved a move to Bakerstown and got me into the work program. And you know the rest." He snuck a glance at me. "So what's your reaction now that you know? Am I off your Christmas card list?"

I laughed, wondering how a man could go through all that and not have residual scarring. "I don't send Christmas cards. The store does though, and if you want, I'll get you on that list. You just have to buy a book from us."

"I appreciate that." He rubbed his face. "You're the third person here I've told about my past. Darla, Barry, and now you. It gets easier with each telling."

I saw Greg walk into the darkened room and figured he'd found out through official channels what Matt had just told me. I patted his arm. "Your past doesn't change who you are now. Don't forget that."

Something in my tone made him look up at me, then at the door. He put the cords down and stood. "I don't think your boyfriend is here on a social call. It sucks to be the easy answer to all the problems in the world just because you're on probation for one stupid action."

"He'll be fair. You know him." I just hoped my words were accurate. Sometimes Greg had too much evidence to look at the emotion of the situation. Which usually worked in his favor, but today, it might work against him.

We watched Greg approach and he caught my eye. "Jill, will you excuse us? I have official business with Matt."

"You just want me to walk away? You know he didn't kill Barry." The words were out before I could stop them.

He looked at me, sadness in his gaze. "I know only a few things. Like Barry is dead and Matt was one of the last people to see him alive." He ran his hand through his hair. "Jill, I'm just trying to do my job here."

"It's okay, Jill," Matt said with a touch of tenderness to his voice. "I want to tell Greg everything. Besides, this time, I didn't do anything wrong. I have nothing to hide."

I drained my beer and threw it away in a trash can as I was leaving. Turning back to watch the men talking, I realized I felt bad for the young boy who had finally found his way and his home but who might lose it for something out of his hands.

I thought a lot as I walked back to my house, and when I arrived, a new car was sitting in Esmeralda's driveway. She was a busy lady. Her words came back to me then: "You'll never find what you're looking for until you look for something else."

I hadn't been looking for the answer I got from Matt. But now that I'd removed him from my suspect list, the only one left was Tiny. I needed to find out more about the six-foot-two chef who created dishes for a small diner in a small town like a chef in a five-star restaurant.

I went inside and opened up my laptop. Google Investigations R Us could be my business name if I ever decided to become a real private investigator. I started with Diamond Lille's website and tried to find everything I could about the chef named Tiny. Two hours later, I closed the laptop and leaned back in my chair in disgust. Nothing. I'd found nothing. Before or after the brief mention of Tiny Colsen on Diamond Lille's website, there had been nothing. Either Tiny wasn't his given name (which was a strong possibility) or Tiny hadn't done anything in his life that had gotten him noticed by the Internet bots. No articles, no Facebook page, no Internet footprint at all.

Emma snored at my feet. It was still early, though the light was dimming, but I had time for the one thing that would help everything that happened this day make sense. I had time for a run on the beach with my favorite partner.

I went upstairs to change into running clothes and Emma sat by the door whining while she watched me get ready. The dog loved to run. Typically, we ran in the morning when the beach was empty. Doing it this late meant she'd have to stay on her leash the entire time, but I knew the dog wouldn't mind. A leash run was better than no run at all.

As I suspected, the beach was packed. We started jogging as soon as we got down the stairs but it was a slow process. We swerved to avoid a family coming up from a day at the beach. The kids, cranky from the sun and surf, were stomping their way through the sand, not wanting to leave. The mother, with a bag filled with wet towels and other beach toys, was leading the way, calling after the kids like they were baby ducks. The dad was in the rear, picking up the lost sandals and blow-up toys. For not the first time, I felt blessed that all I had to do was clean up after my dog.

The mayor had tried to get a "no dogs allowed" sign on the beach, but so far, the council had vetoed his idea. Mostly because a lot of the council members had dogs that they liked to bring with them on their own beach excursions. The mayor didn't have any pets at all. Not even a gold fish. That told you something about the man, didn't it? I thought that should be a mandatory question on any politician's request to run for office. What pets did they have?

I dodged a trio of surfers coming up from the waves, their wet bodies glistening in the sun and their surfboards dangerous to passersby.

"Looks like you picked the wrong time to run," a familiar voice called out to my left. Looking over, I saw Carrie from the diner sitting on a towel with a book in hand. I moved toward her and plopped down on the sand next to the towel.

"It's crazy busy for a weekday." I glanced at my watch. "And it's after five. I would have thought most of the tourists would have left by now."

"Oh, they have. This is mostly town regulars." Carrie waved at the young girl playing in the surf with a bodyboard. Carrie pointed to her. "That's my Hannah. My daughter's oldest. I've been drafted as her beach buddy for the summer as Sarah works in town. We come out here after I get out of the diner. I get to read, she gets to play. It's a good system."

"What are you reading?" I glanced at the cover. "I love that author but I haven't read that book yet."

"I bought it over at your store if you're wondering." Carrie tucked a bookmark in the pages. "That girl you have working afternoons? She suggested the first one and I've been hooked ever since. She got Hannah into some mystery series too. The girl can sell books, that's all I have to say."

"Sasha knows her stuff." I loved hearing that she was doing a great job, even if I already knew it. "Can I ask you a question?"

"I didn't kill Barry."

The frankness of her answer surprised me for a second and it must have shown on my face.

She laughed. "Girl, don't you know you already have a reputation for figuring out who the killer is long before that lovely young man of yours."

"I wouldn't say that." I pulled the leash close and Emma plopped down next to us. "But since you brought up Barry, what do you know about your cook?"

"Tiny? You can't think that man had anything to do with Barry's death. He's a sweetheart. I don't think he even lets a mouse be killed in the kitchen. He bought no-kill traps for the place when we had that problem last year." Carrie shook her head. "Your murder radar is off on this one."

"That's the thing. I don't think he killed Barry, but I can't find anything on a Tiny Colsen. It's like he showed up and started cooking for Lille fully grown." Emma watched a seagull land a few feet from us and I could feel her muscles tense.

"That's because Tiny Colsen isn't his birth name. Once he left wrestling, he started to use his mother's maiden name. I think you'll find what you want to know if you look up Ralph McMasters. He changed his life and I think Tiny fits him better than Ralph, but who am I to judge."

"He wrestled? Professionally?" I shouldn't have been so surprised. With Tiny's body type, he would have been a great athlete.

"Right up until he left six years ago. There was some sort of accident with one of his stunts. The guy felt so bad about actually hurting someone, he quit the sport and went to culinary school. He's been at Diamond Lille's ever since."

As I was running back to the house after my talk with Carrie, I knew one thing. None of the three men who were on the fire training exercise with Barry had killed him. Now, I just needed to prove it and find out who did. The clock was ticking and I didn't have any clue as to what had actually happened.

Chapter 5

Tiny Colsen had led an interesting life before becoming a small-town chef. He'd been big-ish in the world of wrestling. Not a headliner, but a consistent player with a string of wins under his belt. He was loved by the crowds, but apparently, didn't like the grandstanding it took to be one of the really big guys in the sport. By the time Greg came over for dinner, I was still following the Google trail on Ralph McMasters.

Greg started unpacking the groceries he'd bought. "I brought over steaks to grill and potatoes to bake. Or if Doc Ames calls me with the toxicology report and I have to cut the evening short, I bought potato salad so we won't have to wait on the potatoes to cook. He's got it on rush, but you know those guys in the lab."

"I found out some stuff about your suspects. Do you want to know or are you going to give me that lecture where you tell me I'm not an investigator?" Greg didn't like me getting involved in murder cases. He thought it wasn't safe, but I'd been careful and discreet this time. Well, except for going to talk to Matt, but there had been a bartender there so it wasn't like he could have kidnapped me or killed me on the spot. And Greg already knew I'd talked to Matt because he'd caught me.

"I'm going to regret this, but I'll worry if I don't ask. What did you find out?" He grabbed a soda out of the fridge and sat down next to me. For the next ten minutes, I filled him in on what I'd found out. After I was done, he wrote down Ralph McMasters's name in his notebook and then put it away.

"That's all you need?" I closed my notebook and went to season the steaks. "His name? I could be offended."

"You know I don't like you investigating, but everything you've told me I've also found out through official channels. Except Tiny's real name. Every time I go to interview him, he's either left or is coming in late. It's like he knows I'm coming." Greg paused at the back door. "I'll go clean the grill. You want to put those potatoes in the oven? I'm going to take a chance that I'm not going to be called out for the next hour at least."

"I'll get them in and come and join you." I called after him and watched as Emma followed him out. The dog loved him, which was a good thing since he seemed to spend a lot of time at my house. I finished washing the potatoes, sat the steaks in the fridge, and grabbed a glass of iced tea.

Evenings on the porch had been our thing since we'd started dating. I know most girls would want a more "date night" event, but I enjoyed sitting and talking about our days. I stood and leaned against the porch railing, looking out toward the road. Studying Esmeralda's house I noticed another car now sat in her driveway. The woman was fully booked today. I wondered if the spirits got confused in all the commotion. "I got some advice from the other side today," I said to Greg.

"Really? I didn't think you believed in Esmeralda's second sight." He rubbed the back of his neck. "She's always telling me one thing or another. Most of the time, she's spot on, but I think that's more because she's really good at reading people."

"Apparently, she's dreaming my answers." I laughed at the look Greg gave me. "She said she was told I needed to stop looking."

"I so totally believe in her gift right now. She's right. You need to stop looking into things that aren't your business." He grinned and threw Emma's ball into the yard.

"You didn't let me finish. She said I should stop looking and then I'd find what I was actually looking for." I sipped my tea. "And it worked. I couldn't find Tiny on Google so I took Emma for a run. And there was Carrie with my answer."

"I'm not sure it really works like that." He took the slobbery ball from Emma and threw it again, wiping his hand on his jeans afterward. "I like my interpretation better. You should just stop looking."

"So since I'm going to ignore your advice, who are you thinking about as a suspect? Are you sure it was just the four of them? I don't think Matt, Bill, or Tiny could have done this to Barry, do you?"

Greg blew out a breath. "No. I don't. And yes, it was just the four of them. I've asked all of them and they tell me the same story with different versions. Well, except for Tiny. He's still on my list to interview again, but I'm expecting to get the same story. It's not rehashed. They all ring true.

Barry could be a jerk, and they all admit that, but the day he died, no one there had a reason to kill him."

"So what happens if you can't figure it out?" I was afraid I already knew the answer.

Greg stood and paced. "Unless Tiny's past turns out to be a problem, Matt's the one who has the most to lose in that case. He has a serious record. He was the one who found the body. The other guys hadn't gone inside yet. I doubt that there's enough evidence to convict Matt, but the DA might just want to make his life miserable until they have to back off. You know how small towns are. Even if he doesn't go to trial, if the gossip starts, he'll be considered guilty."

"I was afraid you were going to say that."

* * * *

Monday morning, I stopped into City Hall on my way home. Amy sat at the desk, a copy of *Surfer Dude* open in front of her. She didn't even look up when I came into the lobby. Leave it to Amy to buy a magazine with a lot of pictures of hot dudes riding crazy waves and then actually read the articles. "When's your next trip?" I asked her.

"Right after the Fourth of July festival. A group of us are going down to Mexico for a few days. Want to tag along?" Amy turned her magazine over.

"Sun, waves, and hot guys? So not my scene." I plopped down in her visitor's chair. "Did you ever find anything on the changes to the fire regulations?"

"Actually, I was going to stop by this morning, but it got a little crazy here." Amy pulled out a folder with about a three-inch stack of paper inside.

"Yeah, I can tell you've been overrun." I glanced around the empty lobby. "How do you handle the pressure?"

"Stop being a jerk." Amy grinned. "You know I can't leave if there isn't anyone to answer phones, and Esmeralda had an appointment this A.M. so I'm the temporary police dispatcher."

"A doctor's appointment?" I didn't really care, but Amy would know.

She leaned closer. "That's what she told Greg, but she told *me* she had a client insisting on coming in first thing this morning so she had to see them. I guess she had a bad dream and needed it interpreted."

Dreams appeared to be Esmeralda's specialty lately. "Well, thanks anyway for the regulations. I guess I'll take this home to read instead of that new thriller I got this morning."

"No problem. The weird thing is there weren't any new duties or powers given to the fire chief that had been passed through the council. Bill came in a few days ago asking the same questions. I do the notes for the council meetings and went back to check. And Barry asked for more power a few times, but he didn't have the ability to shut a business down unless it was an emergency."

"So he lied to me." Now I really hated the guy, dead or not.

Amy flipped her hair back out of her face. "You and a ton of other businesses. Mayor Baylor was getting a lot of complaints from the community. Darla even came in and sat in his office until he promised to fix the problem."

As I left City Hall, I thought about Mayor Baylor and his promise to correct Barry. Would he have dirtied his own hands to get the fire chief out of his hair and get the complaints to stop? I didn't think so. Besides, it didn't change the fact that there were only three possible killers. Sweet Bill, reformed Matt, and reimagined Tiny. There had to be another person who no one had seen.

My phone rang with the theme song from the *Andy Griffith Show*. I smiled and picked up the call. "Hey, Aunt Jackie, what's going on?"

"You're late for the staff meeting. I know you excused Toby to play policeman, but I expected you as the owner and manager of the place to show up." My aunt's sense of humor was pretty acidic.

"Sorry, I forgot. I'm just down the street. I'll be right there." I turned away from home and power walked to Coffee, Books, and More. Why my aunt couldn't have reminded me before I left the shop this morning, I didn't know. Then I stopped in the middle of the empty sidewalk and took a deep breath. It wasn't my aunt's job to handhold me on this business thing. I needed to do my part. It was, after all, my business. No matter what my aunt thought.

I strolled into the coffee shop and grabbed a cup of coffee before I sat at the table with my aunt, Sasha, and Nick. When I finally sat, I turned toward my aunt. "Did you have an agenda you wanted to cover?"

Eyeing me suspiciously, she handed out a schedule to the three of us. "I want us to get on the same page for next week's festival."

"It's color coordinated. What does yellow mean?" Sasha grinned at the page. "I color coordinate my planner at home. Family time, work time, study time, they all have their own colors."

"Well, this is kind of like that, but yellow means the shop and pink is the annex down by the bicycle shop." My aunt used her copy to indicate the two different schedules.

"Why did you use pink? You could have had a more gender-neutral color, like lime." Nick squirmed in his chair a bit. "I have to hang this up in my room so I can see it while I'm working on my summer projects. And it's pink."

"The color doesn't matter. Anyway, you can see that there are two columns for each day. The yellow is for who will be at the shop and the pink is who is at the annex. Nick, you'll do most of your time at the annex with either Jill or Sasha helping. I'll be stationed here with Amy and Sasha. Jill, you'll fill in where we have holes or where the most business is."

My aunt laid out a set of walkie-talkies. "And we'll keep in touch with these."

Nick picked one up. "Whoa, are these antiques?"

"No. They aren't antiques. They are walkie-talkies. Haven't you ever seen one before?" Aunt Jackie looked between Nick and Sasha, who were both looking at the items like they were an ancient set of drums they were supposed to use to communicate.

"I don't understand. Why don't we just use our cell phones to call when we need help?" Sasha looked at Aunt Jackie like she'd been asked to wash clothes in the river using rocks.

"Well, what if you don't have your phone . . ."

Sasha and Nick both shook their head.

"I would always have my phone." Nick looked at Aunt Jackie like she was speaking a foreign language.

"Well, what if the battery ran out?" My aunt was still trying to sell the advantage of using the radios.

Nick dug in his backpack. He held up a slim metal rectangle. "Then I'll plug it into this and recharge it."

"Ooh, can I see that? I've been meaning to get one, but they're so pricy." Sasha reached for the item and Nick handed it to her.

"Actually, these are cheap at school. I can get you one when I go up next month to sign up for classes. They should have one at your bookstore though."

"That's where I looked. They were over thirty dollars. I figured I'd just be good at keeping the phone charged at night and when I'm driving." Sasha handed the battery charger back.

"I got this for ten bucks. I'll pick you up one. It's always nice to have a backup, just in case." Nick tucked it into his backpack and turned back to the table. Noticing my aunt staring at the two of them, he blushed. "Sorry, I didn't mean to hijack the meeting."

"Getting back to next week. If you start to get slammed, reach out to the other location. You can use the walkie-talkies or call. I don't care." Aunt Jackie paused and looked at each one of us before continuing. By the time she was finished with her meeting, I was worn out.

Nick was the first to leave. "Mom's been in the bakery for days now, getting ready for the festival. I told her I'd help her do some deliveries this afternoon."

It was way past my lunch time and my stomach was growling. I watched Nick leave and Sasha head back to the coffee bar with our cups. I turned to my aunt. "I'm heading to Lille's to grab a bite. You want to come along?"

"No, I've had my share of eating out this week." My aunt picked up a walkie-talkie. "Am I as obsolete as these seem to be?"

"You are not obsolete. You're a classic." I got a smile out of her with that description. "These were from another time when telephones were all landlines. Now, everyone carries a mini computer around with them that also takes phone calls and pictures."

"The world's changing fast. And I'm not ready to get on that moving sidewalk, not just yet." My aunt took the walkie-talkies and put them behind the counter. "You go on and have a nice lunch. We'll talk later."

I left, but my aunt's sadness seemed to follow me to Diamond Lille's. As Carrie brought my tea, she whistled. "What has your goat, missy?"

"My goat?" I glanced up from the menu I knew from heart but didn't know what I wanted yet.

Carrie took the menu from me. "You're in a funk. I know just the meal to get you out of it."

"I don't know . . ."

But Carrie didn't listen to my half-hearted objection, walking away and greeting another table while she ignored me.

I grabbed a book out of my tote and pushed aside the fire regulation file. I could read that later. Like tomorrow later. Or next month later. Or at least before my aunt hired her electrician to fix the problems at the shop that may or may not even be problems. I made a promise to start reading as soon as I got home. I opened the thriller and got lost on the narrow streets of Italy.

Carrie dropped my food off and I nibbled on fish and chips while I read. When I realized the basket was empty, I glanced at my watch. It was close to two and the diner was nearly empty.

When I put the bookmark into the novel and sighed, I knew I'd open it back up as soon as I got home. Fire regulation study would have to come tomorrow. I smiled as Carrie came back with my check. "How do you know exactly what I need?"

"You're easy. You get this small smile when you're eating certain foods. Your pal Amy is the same way. But some folks, like that Josh Thomas, I can't tell if he likes or hates his meal. He pays me the same tip every time, exactly twelve point five percent." Carrie lowered her voice. "Of course that Barry guy made me rethink everything I knew about him when he came in last week. He left me a one hundred dollar tip. For a fifteen dollar lunch! I told him it was too much, and he just shook his head and said it was mine now. Then he walked out. Can you believe that?"

"Weird. Was he always a good tipper?" Maybe I needed to study the victim more and forget about the suspects, who I didn't think could actually be real suspects.

Carrie barked out a laugh. "Not on your life. I can list off a ton of times he stiffed me out of any tip at all. Now, with the kids sometimes I expect that since some of them aren't raised right. But he knew better. I guess maybe that hundred dollars was his way of making up for all the times he left me nothing."

"Maybe." I wondered if Barry was in an atoning mind-set last week and, if so, why. I glanced toward the kitchen. "Hey, could I talk to Tiny for a second?"

Carrie glanced around the empty dining room. "Lille ran to the bank so I think you have about ten minutes before she gets back. Get in and out because if she finds you in there, I'm not saying I let you go back."

Smiling, I grabbed my tote and dropped a few bills on the table for my meal. "I'll be quick. Thanks, Carrie."

"I don't know what you're thanking me for. Time's wasting, tick tock." She started to clean the table and pocketed the bill and the cash to take to the register.

I made my way through the empty tables and, glancing at the door, circled around the counter and right into the kitchen. No one was there, but a door was open to the back. I went out the doorway and there sat Tiny on a folding chair in the alleyway, smoking a cigarette. I sat on the steps going down to the alley and smiled. "Mind if we talk for a minute?"

"Your boyfriend's been trying to corner me for days. Might as well talk to you." He grinned and I realized he had a gold tooth. "What do you want to know besides I didn't kill Barry?"

"Tell me about that morning. Was there anyone else there in the building when you guys showed up at the site?"

Tiny shook his head. "Not that I saw, but I was the last one to get there. I live in Bakerstown so it takes me a while to get here. Barry called this stupid training exercise at six that same morning. I had to be in South Cove by ten. And I'm not much of a morning person."

"So you arrived at ten and the other men were already there?"

"Ten thirty. Man, Barry was hot. He looked like he was already sweating from the heat. *And* he looked tired. If he hadn't got up at the crack of dawn to call us all, he could have gotten more sleep. Anyway, Barry gave me a good dressing down for being late, and then he told us about the exercise. He'd already set up the burn spots, so he was going into the building to light the accelerant. We were supposed to wait thirty minutes, then go in, put out the fire, then tell him what actually caused the fire."

I waited as he put out his cigarette and lit another one.

He laughed as he looked at it. "I wondered if he was going to use a cigarette fire since he was always on my butt about smoking. He said I got enough smoke in my lungs from the work we did and I shouldn't press fate."

"So what did you do while you waited?"

He rubbed his free hand over his bald head. "Bill set a timer on his watch. He has a set process for everything. I teased him that he was being a little OCD, but he just grinned and said, 'Barry told us thirty minutes. I don't want to be late.'"

He paused, flicking an ash into a soda can.

"I guess then we bull . . ." He paused and changed his word. "We talked until the watch went off, grabbed our gear, and put out the fire. It wasn't easy. That building was old and the wood dry like a summer day. We got it out, went inside to find the starting point, then Matt found Barry."

"Matt found him?" I prompted.

"Came running out of the building, ripped his mask off, and then threw up by the tree. I don't think that boy has ever seen a dead body before." Tiny shook his head. "He'll never forget this one."

"Then what?"

"After we got Matt calmed down, he told us Barry was in the building, dead and half burned up. Bill called the police station and I went inside to see if Barry was really dead or if this was just part of the exercise. The boy wasn't exaggerating." He shook his head and put out the half-smoked cigarette. "I'll never forget that sight either."

Chapter 6

"Seriously Jill? What are you doing here?" Greg's voice came from behind me. I glanced up and saw him standing at the doorway.

"Now, mister, don't be getting the wrong ideas. The girl and I were just comparing recipes." Tiny Colsen stood and stared at Greg. "No need for you to get your panties in an uproar."

"And there's no need for you to lie for her. I know you were talking about Barry's murder." He stepped around me and pulled me to my feet. "You go home. I'll interview Tiny because that's my job."

I started up the steps, then glanced at Tiny. "Can I get through the alley to the street?"

"Of course." He turned and pointed behind him. "Main Street's right out there. You avoiding Lille?"

"I'm always avoiding Lille." I smiled at Greg. "Come by the house when you have time. I have a cheesecake."

"You're in enough trouble that it better be chocolate." He squeezed my arm and nodded toward the street. He lowered his voice. "I'll stop by later."

"Thanks for the recipes, Tiny." I grinned as I walked by. "It was nice to talk to you."

"I'll come by that shop of yours soon. I guess I better start buying my reading material there as I'm part of South Cove now." Tiny grinned at me as I walked by.

There was no way this guy was a killer. Which just took all the suspects off my list. And probably Greg's list in the next ten minutes. I wondered if Greg was right. Would the DA push to run a case against Matt just because of his history? The thought troubled me long after I arrived at home.

I put the folder of fire regulations on the coffee table, grabbed a soda, and curled up with the novel I'd started in the diner. I might as well finish it now. I'd do the other reading tomorrow morning when I was really at work. Of course, as a small-business owner, I was always on the clock because I was always thinking about the business.

Right.

I opened the book and got lost in the story.

* * * *

Since Greg hadn't shown up last night, I'd been able to finish the book before I'd crawled into bed late. When I arrived at the store the next morning, I pulled the stack of papers out of my tote. Now I had no excuse not to dig into the fire code. I'd made my way through half of the regulations, highlighting the ones that actually pertained to my store and trying to match those up against Barry's list. I had better luck when I looked at the list that Aunt Jackie's electrician had made. It looked like we were going to have to invest in some upgrades for the building. I poured a cup of coffee and stood staring at the pile of papers.

A woman came into the store and beelined to the coffee bar. "Can I get a double shot mocha with whipped cream? I'll be looking at books too, but right now, I need a jolt."

"Sure. If you want, I can just wait and charge you for all of it together." I moved toward the coffee machine and grabbed a to-go cup. "You want a large in one of these? Or our more upscale in-store china cups?"

"Paper is fine, and yes, as large as you have." The woman sat down at the counter and pulled out a tissue. She wiped her eyes and then blew her nose. "Sorry, I'm dealing with something."

"No worries. It's just you and me here." I handed her the mocha. "I've been going over some upgrades we're thinking about for the store so I needed a break too. What do you like to read? Maybe I can make some suggestions."

The woman picked up one of the sheets of paper on the counter. "Ugh, fire safety codes. My ex-husband used to work in that field." She closed her eyes and I could see she was trying to hold back the tears. "Stupid jerk. I thought I was done crying about him when the divorce was final. Now I'm back to blubbering."

"I'm sorry. Has something happened?" I had a feeling I knew just who was sitting in my coffee shop, wiping away tears, but I could be wrong.

"He died. Recently." She wiped away the tears from her cheeks. "You probably knew him. I'm Heidi Gleason. My ex was Barry."

"I'm so sorry for your loss." I wasn't sure what else to say. I'm never good at these types of conversations. But luckily for me, Heidi didn't seem to notice my hesitation.

"It wasn't like this was unexpected. He'd called last month with the news, told me I'd be losing my gravy train alimony check but that he'd taken care of the kids." She laughed, a short bitter sound. "He hated paying me alimony, even though I'd supported him for years while he went to school. Sometimes men can be such jerks. The good news is I still had a life insurance policy on him that he didn't know about. I'll be able to finish school."

"What are you talking about?" This entire conversation had taken a turn I hadn't expected. Small towns, you never knew who you'd run into. Then her words hit me. "Wait, he called last month? How did he know he'd die in a fire last month?"

She sipped her mocha. "Barry never did have good luck. The fire was just the last straw. Barry had pancreatic cancer. The doctors told him he had only a few months left to live. Of course, I thought he was just being Barry and I didn't believe him until he pulled out his pile of medical bills. I guess I'm going to have to handle all of that now too. Do you know anyone over at city hall? I'm heading there next to see what kind of benefits Barry had."

I gave her Amy's name and number since South Cove didn't really have a human resource department. Then as she looked around at books I texted Greg. Did you talk to Mrs. Gleason yet? She's here in my shop.

I didn't have to wait long for a reply. How do you get involved in these things? I'm out of town right now. Get her cell and text it to me. She was supposed to come straight to the station when she got into town.

That had to be the longest text I'd ever received from him. When Heidi came to the counter with a stack of books, I gave her Greg's message and texted him her number. As she left the shop, she turned back. "You better take care of that man of yours, dear. You never know when something bad could happen, especially with his job."

Sasha came into the shop as Heidi was leaving. She walked behind the counter and stashed her purse. "Who was that?"

I filled her in on Barry's ex-wife's visit, and then a weird idea came to mind. I'd read it in a book recently, but didn't know if it was true or not. Only one way to find out. I grabbed my purse. "Sorry to run so fast, but I'm going to Bakerstown to talk to Doc Ames. If Greg comes in, tell him I'll be back at the house by five."

"Do I tell him where you've gone?" Sasha sipped her coffee, watching me. I shook my head. "Errands. Tell him I went to run errands."

"You may want to stop at the store then before you come back just so you have real proof. Plausible deniability." Sasha grinned. "You are so fun to work for. I never know what kind of trouble you're going to get into next. I just don't want you teaching your mad skills to my daughter. She's crafty enough as it is."

"Nothing wrong with a curious mind," I called back as I left the shop. I had to run home, get my car, and then get into Bakerstown before Doc Ames closed the funeral parlor for the day. He liked taking a short nap in the afternoon.

Since I had to stop at the store afterward and didn't think Doc Ames would appreciate me bringing Emma, I had to leave her at the house. I liked bringing my dog along on car trips. That way when I'm talking to myself, she looks like my intended target. Today, I'd just have to look crazy as I worked out the details of what happened to Barry and the questions I wanted to ask Doc Ames.

His car was still parked behind the building when I reached Bakerstown. "Lucky girl," I muttered as I made my way through the ornate waiting rooms and lobby, back to his office. The place always felt heavy to me. And a little bit creepy. But the funeral director and county coroner was just about the nicest guy you'd ever meet.

I knocked on the door and peeked my head into the office. He was sitting at the desk, reading a file. "Hey, can I come in?"

A wide smile covered his face and he waved me in, sitting the file on his desk. "Do you want some coffee? I made a pot just a little while ago and I told myself I'd stay here working until its gone."

"Sure. Black is fine." I settled into the visitor's chair and glanced around the room. It never changed. Piles of papers covered every surface, except the desk, and they were starting to encroach there as well. I worried that someday I might come in and the paper would have taken over and our Doc would be lost in the piles.

"What brings you here, as if I didn't know already?" He tapped a gnarled finger on the folder he'd been reading. "Such an interesting case, don't you think? Kind of a locked-room mystery. Four men go in, three come out. It would make an excellent movie."

"You know Greg doesn't like me 'investigating.'" I made air quotes around the word. "But I have a couple of general questions for my own curiosity."

He leaned back in his chair, the white hair he wore too long and messy contrasting with the dark worn leather. "And I'm curious to know what you've come up with. I guess we're both rebels. Ask your questions, and I'll tell you what I can without violating my friend's rights."

"This is a general question. If a person died of, let's say, a heart attack, and then the body was burned in a fire, could you determine that?"

"It would depend on how long the body was exposed to the heat. Sometimes the fire is so hot, there are just ashes to work with." He steepled his fingers. "Are you considering a new line of work?"

"Oh, no. Too gross for me. But I have another question." I bit my bottom lip, wondering if I could phrase it correctly to get me the information I wanted. My "source" was very specific on what he'd talk about. "If a person overdosed, then was burned in a fire, is the answer the same?"

He nodded. "Exactly. You have to have a body to be able to test. Sometimes the ashes mix in with the materials around the body and you can get all kinds of crazy readings."

"But Barry's body wasn't just ashes, was it?"

This time he glanced at the folder on his desk. "I don't see the harm in answering that question, so I will. No. Barry was badly burned but that wasn't what killed him."

I leaned closer, sure I had the answer now. "Do cancer patients get high-dosage pain killers?"

Before he could answer, there was a knock on the door. Greg came in to the room. He put a hand on my shoulder as he stood behind my chair. "Doc Ames, I was wondering if I could have a minute of your time."

"Uh-oh, we've been found out, Jill. Your man is on to our wicked secret romance." The older man smiled. "Coffee, Greg?"

"That would be great." He slipped into the chair beside me. "What were you two talking about? Wait, can I guess?"

"I didn't ask specifically about Barry. I was asking hypotheticals." Well, except for that last question. I sipped my coffee. No way was he going to make me feel guilty about this when I had it figured out. "To catch you up, here's what I've found out so far."

Greg listened as I recited the questions and Doc's answers. When I got to the last question, Doc piped in. "And that's where we were. Which I think is a very interesting question. Yes, some patients in cancer treatments get pain killers. And I suspect a patient with a terminal diagnosis might have some pretty strong ones."

Turning toward me, Greg draped an arm around the back of his chair. "Okay, Nancy Drew, what's the solution to the problem?"

"You mean, who killed Barry?" I didn't know if he wanted me to continue the hypothetical discussion or get to real facts.

He shook his head. "Go ahead, let's hear it."

"Okay then, let's put the clues together. Aunt Jackie saw him at the doctor's offices building. I know that there are quite a few cancer doctors in that building because I had a friend who did her chemotherapy treatment there."

When neither one of them spoke, I kept going. "Then he pulls together an impromptu training for three of his volunteers. The three he wanted you to suspect of killing him. Bill, who has been trying to block him at the council meetings. Matt, who has a checkered past anyway. And Tiny, who, well, isn't really Tiny and has a secret. He sets up the fire, makes sure only those three people are in the suspect pool, then goes in and lights the fire."

"Go on." Greg watched me as I scooted to the edge of my seat while I talked.

"Then he takes the meds. But it has to be enough to overdose on. Tiny said he was looking tired, like he could have used more sleep, but maybe he took the pills early, and then when Tiny didn't show up on time, he almost blew the whole plan." I looked from Doc to Greg. "He'd already told his ex-wife that she was losing her alimony. I bet when you look at his finances, he increased his life insurance."

Greg nodded. "Two weeks before the fire."

I fell back into my chair and stared at him. "You were already looking at this theory. You knew Barry tried to set his death up as a murder."

He grinned. "I'd asked Doc for the toxicology because his physical autopsy showed that Barry was dead before the fire happened. He didn't have any smoke damage to his lungs. Which meant none of the three could have killed him. They were each other's alibi's. Tiny even said Bill timed the burn on his watch to follow Barry's instructions to the letter. I think Barry didn't realize he'd ruined his own plot twist."

"You just let me investigate even though you knew there wasn't a murder?"

Greg shrugged. "I figured it couldn't hurt. There wasn't a killer to get nervous about you asking questions. You were completely safe."

"Sometimes you are a real pill, Greg King."

Chapter 7

We'd closed down the coffee shop at seven but Nick would keep the booth open until the fireworks started. He was selling more water and cookies than coffee. I sat at a table near the booth and fingered the red checked tablecloth. Real fabric. Darla had gone all out. Now that her man wasn't under suspicion for murder, she'd dove into the setup and planning. Now, all there was left was the grand finale, fireworks. The band that was currently playing would step down and a DJ would handle the music for the production.

"Nothing to do now but eat and enjoy." Greg took a chicken leg out of the bucket that sat at our table. He still wore his uniform, but I could see he'd shut off the cop persona for the night.

"You don't have to be available for patrolling?" I finished off the watermelon I'd been snacking on all day and pulled the bucket closer to see what was left.

"That's why I'm the boss. Toby and Tim are taking a break too. We have the temps from Bakerstown if something goes south." Greg pulled me close. "I am so glad last week is over. Hell, I'm glad last month is over. It's been crazy."

"Did Mrs. Gleason decide on a funeral?" I hadn't seen the woman in town since our first meeting.

"Actually, there won't be services. His kids and family are doing something next weekend but it's private. I guess they figured with the way he went out, a small event would be better." Greg set the chicken leg down. "I don't know about Barry's choices. It seemed like he wanted to make a wave leaving."

A shadow fell over the table. I looked up and saw Tiny standing there with a couple of baskets of food from Diamond Lille's booth.

"Thought you two might like some chicken wings and shrimp poppers." He grinned as he set them down on the table. "My treat. I'm glad to see you are still talking to each other. I was a little worried from the looks you guys were giving each other the last time I saw you."

"Greg overreacts." I grabbed a popper and dunked it into Lille's special sauce. The crunchy bite was perfect. "These are tasty."

"I don't overreact when you keep your nose out of my business and just deal with your bookstore and coffee shop." Greg took a big whiff of the chicken wings. "I can smell the heat on these. Thanks, man."

"No problem. I'm just glad you all handled the nastiness that happened last week. I can't believe that man would have tried to set any of us up that way." Tiny shook his head. "Some people just don't have a heart, you know?"

I thought that was a perfect description of the Barry I'd met. Maybe he had been a nice guy at some point, but he turned out to be a royal pain. The only thing he'd done with this meanest act was bring the rest of us together. I guess that was going to have to be his legacy.

Tiny held out his hand to shake Greg's. "Anyway, I'm thankful that it's taken care of now. I know Lille and Carrie know my past life, but I'd rather that it not be broadcast to everyone in town. I'm still trying to deal with the memories of that time. I wasn't a very nice guy."

"You were acting." I didn't understand Tiny's pain, but I could see it was real.

He shook his head. "Actions have consequences. Even when they are just part of the job. I'll get over it, someday. For now, I just want to lose myself in my cooking."

"And we love the food you create." I squeezed his arm. "Thanks for coming to South Cove. You're a big part of why I love the town."

Or at least his food was, since I ate way too many meals at Diamond Lille's as part of my normal routine. As he walked away, I noticed Greg scanning the crowd, his attention stopping at the bandstand. I turned my head to see what had caught his attention.

Darla and Matt stood over near the bandstand, watching the crowd. I caught his eye and he waved. They made their way over to the table. "Jill, Greg, isn't the festival great? Darla's outdone herself again."

Darla blushed and swatted his arm. "South Cove festivals are a result of everyone working together. That's why they're always so successful. There's no way I could have pulled this off by myself."

"Whatever you say, goofball." Matt leaned down and kissed the top of her head. An action that made me misty eyed. "The band's almost ready to take a break, so I'm playing DJ, but I wanted to thank you for putting this Barry thing to bed so quickly. I know I might have been an easy target in that whole situation."

"No one would suspect you of doing something like that." Darla looked up into Matt's face.

"Well, it all worked out in the end." Greg jumped into the conversation before it got sidelined.

I'd never heard Matt talk so much. Darla, yes, I was used to not getting a word in edgewise. Maybe that's why they got along so well together. "I'm glad nothing crazy happened in this whole thing."

"Thanks to you." Matt nodded, not breaking eye contact with me. "You were like a dog with a bone. I'm so glad you found the evidence to clear me."

"Hey, what am I? Chopped liver? You realize you were never charged in the case, right?" Greg's voice held a tint of amusement.

"Not for lack of circumstantial evidence. You all could have just seen what I was and not looked at what I've become. And for that, I'm eternally grateful." Matt shook Greg's hand and then squeezed mine. "If I can do anything for either of you, let me know."

"Maybe you could play a slow song so I could dance with my favorite girl before the fireworks."

"I don't think the police department approved a street dance." I grinned at him. "We might be violating a law or something."

"I'll take the risk."

Darla kissed both of us on the cheek. "You two are so cute. We've got to go. The band is getting restless."

I watched them walk away, hand in hand. "Darla says he's happy his past is out and not a secret anymore. He feels like he's home."

"Well, Barry tried to make the California State Pen Matt's new home. I can't believe he tried to frame him." Greg sipped his lemonade. "He had to be out of his mind to plan something like this."

My response was delayed as Bill and Mary stopped by our table.

"We're sitting across the way with your aunt and Josh. Why don't you join us?" Mary gave me a quick kiss on the cheek. I loved the woman, mostly because she kept my aunt happy and occupied as a friend. That meant I didn't have to go on the escapades my aunt enjoyed, like visiting wineries or art galleries.

"We're actually having some couple time." Greg stood and shook Bill's hand. "You know how hard it is to get any private time in jobs like ours."

"And we're here interrupting." Bill smiled down at me. "I do apologize, but I wanted to thank you for dealing with the Gleason thing. If the investigation had gone on through the festival, it would have put a mark on quite a few people's enjoyment of the holiday. Now that it's over, we can all relax."

"Bill, that was insensitive of you. I'm sure Barry's family isn't enjoying the festival this weekend." Mary narrowed her eyes at her husband.

"All I meant was there are a lot of people who might have been considered suspects if these two hadn't solved the case so quickly." He rolled his eyes. "It was a compliment, dear."

"Men." Mary snorted, then turned back to me. "Anyway, I just wanted to stop by and let you know where we are, just in case."

"I think we're good."

As they walked away, I glanced at Greg. "Time to ourselves?"

"I'm getting a little annoyed at being interrupted every few minutes. Maybe we should go hang out in your shop or on the roof. We could see the fireworks there." Greg looked hopeful. "And we have plenty of food to get through."

I was considering the idea when I realized I hadn't answered him about Barry's intentions. Besides, I needed to be close, just in case Nick needed me. I decided to change the subject.

"Maybe he wanted to go out on his own terms. Barry didn't seem like the type of guy who would want to go quietly into the night. And if the cancer was progressing, he might not have had an opportunity to die on the job soon enough. I'm not sure when the last fire in town was." I leaned on Greg's shoulder. "It's just sad."

"He could have volunteered for one of the wild fire crews. I'm sure they've been going out this summer. I'm just ticked off that he did it here, where I had to deal with the aftermath." Greg ran a hand through his hair. "Whatever doesn't kill us . . ."

Greg didn't finish the saying as Sasha plopped down next to me. She handed me a fluff of cotton candy. "Thanks."

"I was wondering if you needed me for the rest of the night. Olivia is with her grandmother in Bakerstown and I thought I might head down to the beach and the carnival. I'm a big fan of the rides." Sasha grinned as she tucked a wad of the sugary pink blob into her mouth.

"Sure. Nick can handle closing. If you want some company, I saw Kyle walking through here earlier. Maybe you can find him." I put on my best innocent smile.

Sasha shook her head. "You never give up, do you? Anyway, I already have a partner in crime."

Toby walked up behind her. He glanced at Greg. "I've got my cell if you need me. I'll be down at the beach."

"You're free until after the fireworks. I told you that already." Greg studied the two. "Traffic control is going to be a bear. It's probably better you're down at the beach to deal with people getting out of the parking lot and onto the highway."

"I'll check in as soon as the fireworks are ready." Toby put a hand on Sasha's shoulder and leaned down. "What about you? Are you cleared?"

"Definitely." Sasha stood and took Toby's hand. "I'll see you Tuesday morning for my shift."

I waited until they were out of earshot. "Didn't see that coming. Did you?"

"Not at all. But you know Toby, he's kind of a flake. I hope Sasha doesn't have big plans for the future." Greg moved the food toward the middle of the table and scooted toward me. "I'll give it a week."

Watching them walk down the street toward the beach, I sighed. "I don't know. This feels different than Toby's other relationships."

"Let's just let them be for a while." Greg pulled me closer. "I'd rather talk about us."

Relaxing into the music, I glanced around at the festival. Families were laughing and kids were playing with sparklers even though their parents were calling after them. Everyone was having fun. It was a good day and a great festival.

"Happy Fourth of July," Greg whispered in my ear as he pulled me closer on the bench.

And as I leaned into him, I realized it *was* a happy day. And for a second, I let the gratitude of the moment wash over me. Life right now was perfect and wonderful. Tomorrow's problems could wait until tomorrow. Today I was happy.

Santa Puppy

A Tourist Rap Novella

CHAPTER 1

Home. It's somewhere we can lay our heads at night. Where we can store our belongings and cook our food. Home is where we live with the people we love, raise our children, and cuddle with our pets. Some people live in houses. Some people live in homes. And a few, more than I'd like to admit, live in shelters and on the street, whether they be man or beast. I couldn't do much regarding the human issue of homelessness today, but I'd had a brainstorm about the beast part.

Today, several of my friends and I were going to the Humane Society. With the window open, I could hear the waves crashing on the rocks as Greg King, my boyfriend and South Cove's primary police detective, drove his pickup truck up the Pacific Coast Highway to Bakerstown.

Greg's blond hair was just a little long, and the rushing wind was making him look like one of those models in the slow-motion ads. I'll totally admit it. My boyfriend is a hottie. But his best attribute is a huge heart. He reached over and squeezed my hand. "This is an exciting project. Just think how many pets will be adopted after next Saturday's party."

"What if they're not? It's not fair that they have to be in those cages in the first place. They didn't do anything wrong." My resolve was wavering. Maybe I could bring home at least one small dog. Emma, my golden retriever, wouldn't mind having a new friend.

"Jill, you know you can't save the world. We're going to make those dogs so irresistible that no one will be able to say no." He turned up the volume on the stereo and started humming along with a Christmas carol.

I guess I should introduce myself. I'm Jill Gardner, and I run the only bookstore slash coffeehouse in South Cove. Well, I own the place. My aunt Jackie is the manager and she runs the store—and me, most days. Of all the places I've ever lived, South Cove feels like home. The town is the perfect little tourist spot right off Highway 1. We have one restaurant and a ton of art studios and galleries and a few specialty shops, so if you're looking for coffee and a treat, it's either my place—Coffee, Books, and More—or Diamond Lille's. We have a pretty good hold on the food business. The closest grocery store is in Bakerstown. A fact I'd bemoaned more than once.

"Hey, when we're done at the shelter, can we stop by the store? I need to pick up some things for the house, and I doubt that I'll be this way again before the Christmas party."

Greg nodded reluctantly, which was his usual response when I asked him to go shopping with me. The guy didn't mind cooking dinner, but he hated stepping into the store. I knew I wouldn't have much time once we stopped, so I took out my phone and started making a quick list of what I needed. I'd told Amy I'd be part of her Christmas cookie exchange, so I needed to bake eight dozen cookies before the party on Wednesday. What had I been thinking? And what was I going to do with seven dozen cookies once I got home?

"How many cookies can I bring down to the station on Thursday?" The people who worked for Greg were always looking for free food.

He looked at me, not smiling, but I could see the humor in his eyes even through his sunglasses. "You know Amy will be bringing in her extras. And Sasha's going. She'll bring in some even though Toby's dating Elisa now." Greg sighed. "That guy needs to settle down. I'm tired of the string of women flowing through the station. But that's not my business. Anyway, cookie-wise, you're going to have to be more creative than just dumping them at the station."

"See, this is the problem with being friends with the people you work with. They all have the same oversupply of cookies." I leaned my head back and let my hand hang out the window, playing with the wind currents. "I should have told Amy I was busy that night. Or sick. I *could* be sick and then I wouldn't have to go. No one wants cookies from a sick woman."

"I'll help you make cookies Tuesday night. It will be fun. We can turn on Christmas movies and drink eggnog while we bake." He paused, glancing at me. "Unless you want to ask your aunt to come bake with you. It would be a fun time."

"I don't think Aunt Jackie wants to help. Besides, she works the late shift on Wednesday." Which was a perfectly good excuse for why she'd said no to Amy's invitation. I sighed and checked my phone. No messages. "And she won't let me take her shift."

"She's a mean one, your aunt," Greg deadpanned.

"Not funny. You know she and Harrold are coming to the shelter today to help bathe the dogs. I don't know what she's even thinking. These dogs aren't all teacup poodle–size."

"Your aunt will be fine. She'll handle whatever comes her way. And if the dog she's given is too big, I'll switch her out." Greg turned the car onto the road that would take us to the shelter parking lot. "You're kind of grumpy today. It's a good thing we're going to go work with puppies. Maybe that will cheer you up."

"I'm not grumpy." But even as I said it, I knew it was a lie. I *was* out of sorts. Maybe it was because of the upcoming holiday. Maybe it was because of the cookies. Whatever it was, I was South Cove's version of a scrooge. I took a deep breath and sent the bad juju out of my body with my breath. The positive-mantra trick was one of Amy's suggestions. She was way into the California New Age lifestyle, as long as it didn't affect her surfing obsession. I believed that a bad mood happened and it never hurt anyone. Being sunny and happy all the time just wasn't a natural state of the human condition.

Amy and her boyfriend, Justin, would be joining us at the shelter. I guess I needed to blow off my bad mood before I got there, or she'd be talking to me about figuring out what I've been doing that has messed up my chi, or whatever it was that she thought caused bad moods. Sometimes I wondered why we were best friends. On some levels, we were so different. But maybe those differences were what brought us together.

"Are you going to be able to get off on Saturday to attend the party?" I stretched out on the seat, knowing we were just a few minutes away from our destination. My Jeep was roomy, but Greg's truck cab was crazy comfortable.

"I should be there, unless something goes crazy at the station. You know how things can pop up." He pulled off the highway and onto the road that would take us directly to the shelter on the edge of town.

"We haven't had a dead body pop up in South Cove for a while."

Greg shook his head. "You know I deal with more than just murder in my job, right?"

As we drove through town, I watched out the window as we passed by the streets. A few blocks in, a Santa stood on the street corner. Dressed in the traditional suit with padding, he looked the part. He had to be sweating buckets. But as we passed by, he waved at the truck. "Funny, he wasn't near a store."

"Who wasn't near a store?" Greg glanced toward my side of the street.

I turned around and looked behind us; now I didn't see him at all. Could he have gotten into a car that quickly? "Don't tell me you didn't see the guy dressed as Santa back there."

Greg reached up and adjusted his rearview mirror. "I don't see him now, either."

"I know. That's kind of weird, right?"

"Or maybe you just have too much Christmas stress on your brain. Loosen up and let's have fun this afternoon. No visions of Santa until the actual day." He parked the truck in the front parking lot at the brightly painted building. "I'd love to be able to cheer you up, but we don't even have any open cases for you to stick your nose into this week."

I grinned and unclicked my seat belt. "I know, but I like solving mysteries more when it's not just someone egging old Mr. Williams's house."

"I'll have you know I solved that in record time." He met me on the sidewalk. "Mostly because the kids' parents brought them in and made them apologize after overhearing them bragging."

"See. Murders are much more interesting. Especially the ones around here. Maybe I should start an investigative club and we could go around solving cold cases."

"I think I'd have to shoot you." He smiled as he said it so I knew he was kidding, somewhat. I guess I was pushing some buttons with him too. He knew I'd never set up a club. That would take time away from my favorite pastime, reading.

Before we got further along the path our conversation was going down and possibly into an actual argument, Harrold pulled his electric car into the parking lot. The shelter had a charging station, and as he got out, he plugged the car into the port. "Good morning, children. Are you ready to take on a pack of angry beasts?"

"Now, Harrold, just because they are at a shelter doesn't mean the animals are angry." My aunt pulled on a jacket and tucked her purse into the trunk. She glanced at Greg's truck. "Do you want to put your purse in Harrold's trunk? It would be out of sight."

"No, I'm fine." I didn't want to tell her that I hadn't brought my purse. I had my house keys, my phone, and my debit card. My aunt would freak if she knew I didn't have a makeup case, a brush, an emergency sewing kit, and a stash of medications handy everywhere I went. I figured if I needed something, I could stop at one of the pharmacies that seemed to be on every corner.

Aunt Jackie frowned and glanced toward the truck, but Harrold saved me. "Come on, Jackie, leave the girl alone. If she says she's good, she's good." He took her arm and led her to the sidewalk, locking the car with his remote. He reached out and shook Greg's hand. "Are you still keeping the streets of South Cove safe for the tourist horde?"

"Yes sir. You go on in, we'll follow." Greg squeezed my arm. He liked the idea of Harrold and Aunt Jackie as a couple. He leaned down and kissed my cheek. "I really enjoy your family."

And the really strange thing was he wasn't just saying that. Greg liked Aunt Jackie. Even when she was over-the-top with her sarcasm or pushing her nose into business that she shouldn't be in, he loved me, so he loved—or at least liked—my family. It was a good feeling.

A young woman in a bright pink polo with Bakerstown Shelter embroidered on the pocket was at the front desk. Her ponytail bounced as she stood and greeted us with a cheery, "Good morning and welcome. Are you here for your forever friend?"

"Actually, we're with South Cove's Coffee, Books, and More? We're here to help get the dogs ready for the party on Saturday?" I stepped forward, ready to sign in or whatever they wanted us to do.

"Ellen told me you were coming. In fact, she's back with another couple from your group who just arrived." The woman reached down and keyed something in, then spoke into the headset she wore. "Hey, the volunteers are here. Can I just send them back?"

We waited as the answer came back. She nodded, listening, then took off her headset and walked around the counter. Opening a side door, she pointed to another door at the end of the hallway. "Just go through there and Ellen will meet you at the end of the cages."

We walked down a long white hallway that felt more like a hospital than an animal shelter, but as soon as we opened the next set of doors, we heard the clamor.

Dogs barked and cats meowed, and there were some other noises I didn't recognize. We walked past a row of adult cats who watched us with bored eyes. Cats were that way. *Take me or don't, I serve no human* seemed to be the standard nonverbal message from the felines.

When we walked along a row of adult dogs, the attitude changed. Dogs had a different approach to getting new homes. It was more of a frantic plea of *get me out of here, I'll do anything you want.* I appreciated the desperation in their ploy.

"There you guys are!" Amy waved us over to where she stood with Justin and an older lady. "I was just telling Ellen that you are never late. Especially Jackie."

Aunt Jackie glanced at her watch. "Technically, I'm still five minutes early."

Harrold chuckled. "I'm sure it wasn't a criticism, dear."

I decided to ignore them and held out my hand to Ellen. "I'm Jill Gardner. I'm so happy you agreed to be part of our Christmas celebration this year."

Ellen beamed and squeezed my hand. "Oh, no, you don't understand. We're the ones who are grateful that you chose us to help this year. I know there are so many charities out there, but the shelter kind of gets lost in the bustle of the season. And honestly, we tend to frown on people giving puppies and kittens as gifts. Adding a new member to your family requires time for you to prepare. You don't just get a baby human—you have nine months to get used to the idea."

"That's a good analogy. So, do you want to do adoptions on Saturday?" Now I was confused. Maybe we were rushing things.

"Oh, yes. So many of our older residents are hoping to be rehomed soon. I swear, so many people don't know how to deal with senior dogs and cats. They think just because they need a little more care, it's time to turn them in and get a new animal. It makes me sad." She shook off the emotion. "I didn't mean to make a big deal out of our adoption process, but we want the best for all our residents. We are a no-kill shelter, so we're always full or almost full. Your event might just be able to match up some families with the dog or cat they've been waiting for."

I felt totally confused now, but since we were still on, I'd let Ellen deal with the adoption process.

"Let's get started getting these guys all pretty and smelling good." Greg must have felt my hesitation.

"Sounds like a plan." Justin looked around. "Where do we start?"

Ellen moved the group into the grooming salon, as she called it. As we passed more cages, a small terrier reached out his paw to me.

"Hey, buddy. Are you going to get a bath today and a new home on Saturday? You look like you'd be a great pet." I reached my fingers into the cage and rubbed behind his ears. He leaned into me, then licked my hand. My heart broke. I wanted him. I wanted all of them and I was going to feel this way, over and over, for the next week.

"You're going to be giving someone a very happy Christmas." A man spoke behind me and I turned my head, not wanting to break contact with the dog. An older man with bright white hair and a white beard stood behind me, holding a cocker spaniel.

"You know about our event?" As the words came out of my mouth, I felt stupid. Of course he did. He must work here with Ellen.

"I know about a lot of things." He smiled and rubbed the dog behind its ears. "But that one is special. She has waited a long time for this gift."

I turned toward the dog, who had stopped licking my hand and was now watching the man. "I thought this one was a male dog. Guess I was wrong."

When no one answered, I turned to find the hallway empty. I looked at the card on the cage. Baby was a ten-year-old male terrier. Glancing back at the dog, I cocked my head. "You saw him, right?"

A short bark answered me.

I glanced back down the hallway. Where had he disappeared to so quickly? I was about to go find out when I saw Greg waving at me from the doorway.

"Are you helping or not?" He stepped toward the cage. "This is Baby. He's first on our list. Do you want him? I have a tiny poodle for your aunt."

I nodded as Greg opened the door and Baby jumped into my arms.

"I guess he likes you." Greg smiled and turned to the next cage. "Let me get one more and we can get started on the bathing process."

I looked down at Baby, who was now giving me kisses on my chin. "You know I can't keep you, right?"

I swear the dog grinned and I saw the answer in his eyes. He knew I'd have a hard time putting him back in the cage.

The problem was, the dog was right.

CHAPTER 2

I walked over to a table where I'd first brush the dog to get the knots out of his hair, then dump him in the tub. Baby had a short coat, but it was caked in mud. Ellen stood beside me and gave the dog a rub under his chin.

"Baby's new to the shelter. His owner was found dead on the beach last week. It was really sad. The dog never left his side." Ellen sighed as Baby licked the side of her hand. "You miss your guy, don't you?"

I glanced over at Greg. "I'm surprised you didn't know about the death."

"I knew about it. He was found closer to South Cove than Bakerstown." Greg stroked the fur on what appeared to be a husky-poodle mix. "I was called in, but Doc Ames ruled it an unattended death. The guy had a heart attack."

I rubbed Baby's head. "It wasn't unattended, was it, Baby? You were there for your master, weren't you?"

The dog let out a small bark and a wiggle. He acted like he knew exactly what I was saying.

"He's very good at social interaction. If he was younger, he would have been snatched up the first few days he was here. But I'm sure we'll be able to place him soon." Ellen moved on to another table.

I put the holding leash around the dog's neck and realized he had on a collar. "Hey, buddy, let's take this off."

I found the buckle and loosened it. When the collar fell off, so did the backing. I picked it up. "You really need a new collar, Baby. This one's falling apart."

I looked at the two pieces. The front was blue with fake rhinestones and a medal that had a rabies number and last year on the tag. He'd been taken care of, even if his owner had been homeless.

When I went to set the collar down on the table, a key fell out of a rip in the side. The dog put his foot on it in what looked like an attempt to hide it. I gently moved his foot and he growled at me.

Quickly, I pulled out the key and stepped back out of the dog's reach. Baby didn't try to bite, but he was agitated. The key was small and had a number on it. Maybe the prior owner had put his valuables in the bank or a locker and hid the key with his dog. "Hey, Greg? Can you come here a minute?"

He hadn't put his dog up on the table yet, so as he walked over, he carried the husky-poodle mix. Baby barked his disapproval at the other dog's proximity. Greg's dog just ignored the insult and curled closer into Greg's neck. Greg adjusted the dog tighter into his arm. "What do you need?"

Holding up the key so he could see it, I asked, "Is this a safe-deposit key?"

He leaned closer and now Baby growled at the other dog. "Looks like it. Put that in your pocket and I'll do some checking on Monday to see if it matches up with our beach guy. Maybe there's more to his story than just passing away on a beach."

"If he had something or someone, they should be told." I glanced at Baby. "And maybe he'd have a home to go to."

Greg stepped back, absentmindedly rubbing the ear of the dog in his arms. "If I remember, there was no next of kin. Opening the box may give us more information about the guy."

As Greg left to start the bath process for the husky-poodle mix, I slipped the key into my jeans pocket and turned back to Baby. "Let's get you all cleaned up. Maybe your guy had a relative who wants to take you in? You need to be all pretty and look your best, just in case, right?"

Baby barked his agreement.

For the next few hours, my life was a madhouse of one dog after another as we brushed and bathed, then turned the dogs over to the groomer the shelter had hired to cut their fur if needed. Aunt Jackie and Harrold were in charge of the final blow-dry and delivery back to a clean cage with fresh food and water. Thirty dogs later, we were done.

Ellen moved us into a conference room where there were cookies and drinks. I grabbed a bottle of water and motioned her to the side. "Hey, I wanted to tell you that Baby's collar broke apart during the grooming."

"One of the aides has already given him a new one. Don't worry about it. A lot of times they come in with old collars and we just throw them away." She patted me on the arm and started to turn away, but Greg stood on her other side.

"What Jill's trying to say is she found a safe-deposit key in the collar." He held out his hand, obviously expecting me to just hand over the key. While I dug it out of my pants pocket, he continued. "I'm taking it into evidence custody. Do you want a receipt for the key?"

"We wouldn't have found it without you guys, so I guess it's fine." Ellen dropped her voice. "What do you think he had in the box?"

"Now, that is the question, isn't it?" Greg smiled and slipped the key into his pocket. He led me back to the table where Amy was finishing her second cookie. "What's on the schedule now? Anyone up for dinner at the Roundabout since we're out of town anyway?"

"Harrold and I need to get back. We're having dinner with Mary and Bill." My aunt stood, and Harrold, holding a water bottle, joined her.

"Nice seeing you guys." He nodded to the group. "I don't think I've ever washed so many dogs before in my life."

"Stick with us, you'll have all kinds of new experiences." Justin reached out and shook the older man's hand. "See you around town."

"He'll be at the party." Aunt Jackie shook her head. "You all act like we're never going to see you again after we leave."

Harrold leaned down and fake-whispered in Aunt Jackie's ear. "They know we're old and they might not see us again."

Laughing, I gave my aunt and her boyfriend a hug. "What can I say? I guess you raised us to have manners and respect our elders."

Harrold kissed me on the cheek. He turned to Aunt Jackie, but I saw the humor in his eyes. "See, she used the word *elders*. I told you they see us as old."

"Stop teasing the children, Harrold." Aunt Jackie gave me an air kiss. "I'll talk to you on Monday. I'd like to finalize the last-minute preparation items for the party."

"You know where to find me." We hadn't moved to winter hours but would after the Christmas party, which meant I'd be opening the store bright and early for my commuter customers.

After Aunt Jackie and Harrold left, Greg focused on Amy and Justin. "What about you two? Or are you going to hit the waves after this?"

Amy and Justin were crazy-dedicated surfers. It was one of the things that kept them together.

Justin grinned and grabbed another cookie. "You caught us on a break night. I'm taking Amy up the coast tomorrow to chase waves, but we don't have plans tonight. What do you say, Amy? Want to grab some grub?"

She stood and came around the table to stand by Greg and me. "I'm in. But only if you tell us what you were talking to Ellen about."

Greg put a hand on my arm and started leading me toward the doorway. "Sounds like a plan."

We drove a couple of blocks to the restaurant and waited for Amy and Justin to arrive. Greg leaned his head back on the seat's headrest and sighed. "I'm hoping that this only has the guy's personal items. I'd hate for Bakerstown to have to reopen this case."

"But if it leads us to who killed him?" I didn't understand Greg's reluctance.

He shook his head. "Doc Ames was very clear on this. The guy had a heart attack. We looked for another cause with no luck. It wasn't murder."

Amy and Justin parked and we all went into the restaurant together. As soon as we sat down, Amy turned to me.

"Aren't you looking forward to the cookie exchange? I've been testing recipes all week. Do you know what you're bringing?" My friend's face was filled with hope and joy.

Greg coughed into his hand and I kicked him under the table.

"I hadn't really thought about it. Maybe chocolate chip?" I studied the menu, not making eye contact.

"Oh, no, that won't do. It has to be a special cookie. I'll send you over some ideas as soon as I get home. Then you can bake a trial run tomorrow." She keyed a note into her phone. "It's no big deal, you'll love the process."

I already hated the process and was beginning to think that maybe I did have latent Scrooge tendencies in my DNA. My aunt had never been a big Christmas fan, so maybe I was just showing my heritage. I decided to grab a lifeline. "Greg and I are doing the baking on Tuesday night and he wanted to pick out the recipe together."

Amy turned her laser focus from me to Greg and her face softened. "Well, isn't that the most romantic thing I've heard of. I can't even get Justin to talk about his Christmas memories and you two are starting your own traditions."

I watched as my friend wiped a tear from her eye. "Yeah, we're just so excited."

This time the kick I aimed at him was a little lighter and more playful. He reached down and squeezed my thigh, just above the knee. Then he turned his charm on Amy. "We're just two peas in a pod. You know how much Jill loves Christmas. I'm just glad I'm here to help her enjoy the celebrations. Hopefully there won't be any emergencies on Tuesday night. But I'm sure she can muddle through without me if I get called out."

Now I narrowed my eyes. Had he just threatened to leave me alone with all this cookie mess? "I'm sure Toby or Tim can handle any trouble that may occur. You know, everyone has to be good at Christmas or Santa won't bring them presents."

I thought I heard a hearty *ho ho ho* from the lobby and turned my head to check it out. A flash of red dashed across the hall. Blinking, I stared at the now-empty doorway. I felt Greg's hand on my arm.

"Jill? What's going on?" He leaned close and looked in the same direction, seeing nothing.

I shook my head and turned back toward the table and my friends. The waiter had joined us, and his gaze followed ours across the room, a questioning look on his face.

"Sorry, I just thought I saw something." I faked a smile and focused on the menu. I really needed this Christmas thing to be over and done with before I had a nervous breakdown or something. "I'm starving, how about you?"

When we were in the truck on the way home, Greg turned down the music. When he glanced over, I could see the worry in his face. "So what really was going on tonight at the table? Did you see someone you thought you knew? An old friend, maybe?"

"No blasts from the past. I thought I heard a Santa coming into the restaurant, and saw a red coat go by." I talked fast to get the words out.

"Jill," Greg spoke slowly, which made me start to steam, just a bit. "There was no Santa in the restaurant. Maybe you're just seeing Santas because you're so busy with the Christmas party. I promise to make cookies with you on Tuesday. I was just kidding with Amy. Besides, my mom always said I was the best baker out of all her kids."

"I'm sure you're right." But in my mind, I was sure he was wrong. For some reason, Santa was stalking me this Christmas, and I was going to find out why. Even if I had to be naughty to do it.

CHAPTER 3

Trying to get past my Christmas slump, I pulled out the Christmas ornaments I'd stashed in the third bedroom. I thought I'd turn it into a library someday, but Greg kept making comments about my needing a workout room. I thought the shed in the back would work better for that, and for days I didn't want to exercise, the room wouldn't be in my house, making me feel guilty. Out of sight, out of mind.

When I got everything downstairs, I looked at my artificial tree and picked up my phone. "Hey, what are you doing today?"

"I was going to watch a game, why?" Greg was a big football fan. Well, actually, football, basketball, baseball—if it was a team sport, he watched it.

"Can I borrow you and your truck this morning? I'll buy coffee and donuts." I moved the table I had below the front window over to the other side of the room.

"What are we doing?"

Smiling at the now-empty space, I answered, "I need help picking out a tree for the house."

"I thought you had an artificial tree. Strike that, I know you do, I moved it to the second-floor bedroom last summer."

"I want a live tree this year. When can you be here?"

Greg mumbled something that I didn't hear, but when I asked him to repeat it, he said, "I'll see you in twenty minutes. I've got to shower still."

I started unpacking the boxes and had the living room in a huge mess by the time he came in the front door.

"It looks like the elves threw up in here." He walked over one of the piles of garland and into the kitchen with his travel mug. "Let me grab some coffee and I'll be ready. There's a tree lot in Bakerstown."

"Now who's being a scrooge?" I followed him into the kitchen. While he grabbed travel cups out of the cupboard, I let an uncooperative Emma out into the back yard. "You know if we don't take her with us, she'll eat some or all of the decorations."

"Which will mean a trip back to Bakerstown for the vet and more tree-trimming stuff." He poured coffee into the cups. "I'm not taking that chance. Besides, I haven't spent nearly enough time with my girl this week."

"I'd be flattered, but I'm sure you're talking about Emma." I came up behind him and put my arms around his waist.

"Are you?" He turned in my arms, then leaned down and kissed me.

When we came up for air, I stepped back and let Emma in, grabbing her leash from the back door. "You could stay for the day and help me decorate the tree."

"I can stay for a while, but I told Jim I'd meet him at the Locker Room to watch the game. The holidays are hard for him." He looked around the room. "Do you need anything else?"

"Just my purse. I'll go lock the front door and you get Emma in the truck. I'll be out in a second." I headed into the living room. Greg's brother, Jim, had lost his wife a few years ago. Holidays would be hard since everything I'd heard about the woman said she was devoted to her husband and her home. We'd hosted Thanksgiving at my house for the last two years. But Christmas had always been about just us and Aunt Jackie and whoever she was dating. I made a mental note to talk to Greg about inviting Jim as well this year.

If he even wanted to come. The guy didn't like me, as he was still in the pro-Sherry camp and thought his brother had moved too hastily in the divorce. I don't think he liked Sherry all that much, but he was a true believer in marriage vows.

I grabbed my tote and locked the front and back doors behind me. Greg and Emma were already in the truck and they were both watching out the window, waiting for me to join them. Emma might not be our child, but at times we felt like family. I just needed to get over that feeling scaring the crap out of me.

Greg headed the truck onto Highway 1 for the second time in two days. Which reminded me about the key.

"Did you find what the key opened?"

He looked over at me in amusement. "You realize banks are closed on Sunday, right?"

"Oh, yeah." I slumped back into my seat. Baby had carved out a piece of my heart, and it was hard to think of him in that cage, waiting for someone to pick him as their forever pet. "I'm just hoping that there's some extended family who would want to take Baby. It must be hard for him to be with someone for so long and then be all alone."

"He's not alone. There are thirty other dogs in the shelter right now." Greg rubbed his arm. "I'm sure I bathed all of them yesterday."

"You have one in the back who could use a bath and a brush when we get back." Reaching back, I rubbed the top of Emma's head.

"Did you miss the part where I said I was meeting Jim?" He glanced over and grinned at me. "It's a hard life, but someone has to watch the game. The players put so much energy into playing, it would be rude for no one to watch."

"And you are definitely not rude." Smiling, I curled my leg up underneath me. "I'll get her in the bath as soon as I get the living room done. It was on my list anyway. I just thought, since you're such a dog washing professional after yesterday, you might want to show off your talents."

"You were just trying to get out of bathing her. I bet she's heartbroken that you're trying to push her off on someone else."

"Whatever. You know she loves you just as much as me." I leaned forward when I saw the flashing Christmas lights. "Is that the lot?"

"Yep. According to Esmeralda, the lot has been here for over thirty years and is still run by the same woman. She gets her trees out of a small town in Oregon in the mountains. Sherry never wanted a real tree, so I always sent Esmeralda to get one for the station once I moved back here." He grinned as he turned the truck into the parking lot. "Having a real tree is one of the best parts of Christmas."

"Besides the presents." She clicked the leash on Emma's collar.

Greg turned off the engine. "And the cookies."

"You are still on the hook for coming on Tuesday to bake with me. I'll start when I get off my shift, but I expect you to come as soon as you can leave the station." I focused my gaze on him. "Right?"

"Of course." He stared at something over my shoulder, then pointed. "Isn't that the Santa you saw in the restaurant?"

I spun around in my seat, but there was no one there. When I turned back around, Greg had already left the truck and was walking toward the trees. I climbed out of the truck and opened the door so Emma could jump out. "Why do I think I'm going to be baking eight dozen cookies by myself?"

Emma barked as if to say, *Don't worry Jill, I'll be there.* Or more likely, *Let's hurry up and catch Greg. I love Greg.*

My dog was a traitor, through and through.

We caught up with Greg a few minutes later, and he took Emma's leash and put an arm around my shoulder.

"If we weren't in short sleeves and sandals, this would almost feel like Christmas." He kissed me on the top of the head.

"Oh, no. Don't think you're getting out of cookie baking that easily, buddy. Distracting me only works for so long. I would have thought you'd learned that about me by now." I reached out and ran my hand over a tree's needles. They were soft, and the smell that covered my hand was Christmas in a bottle. "This was a really good idea."

"Well, thank you."

I stared at him. "I'm the one who suggested a live tree, not you."

"Yeah, but I knew where the lot was. You only had a vague idea of a tree. I had a workable plan." He pointed to one down the row. "What height were you thinking about?"

"I don't know, lower than the ceiling so I can put an angel on top?"

An older woman pushed through a row of trees and stood next to us on the path. "You're probably going to want a six-footer, then. If you're in a normal house. But if you have vaulted ceilings, the sky's the limit."

I studied the woman. She had a red-checked apron on with a picture of Mrs. Claus as well as what must be the name of the lot: Lumberjack Phil's Christmas Pines. "Do you work here?"

"Yes and no." She grinned. "I'm Beth, I own the place. So at least I don't have to pay myself an hourly wage to wander through the trees and pretend to get lost in the forest. What about you two? This your first Christmas together?"

"Second," Greg said.

"We're not together," I blurted out. Greg stared at me.

"What?" He stepped back and held up his arms. "Did I miss a memo?"

"No, I mean, yes, we're together, but we're not married or living together or anything like that." I could feel the hole I was digging getting deeper. I was definitely baking all by myself on Tuesday. "We're dating."

Amusement twinkled on Beth's face. "Well, you look like the perfect couple. Especially with that dog. I had a beau once. He…well, you're not here to learn about me. Let's get you a tree. Or are you getting two? One for each place?"

"Just one. I'm over at the house more than I'm at my place anyway." Greg nodded toward a large tree in the center of the lot. "Although I may come back and get that one for the station."

She turned back and considered him. "You could be a fireman."

"Police. I run the guys over at South Cove's station. My dispatcher usually comes and gets our tree from your lot." He held out a hand. "Greg King. And this is my girlfriend, whether she admits it or not, Jill Gardner."

As we shook hands, I added, "I own Coffee, Books, and More. It's a..."

"Coffee shop and bookstore, I got it." Beth looked out in the direction of the ocean, though you couldn't see the actual water from where they were. "I don't leave Bakerstown much anymore. I used to love to travel, but oddly enough, this place doesn't support the high life. I do good to pay my bills and have a bit left over for food and the essentials."

"Where did you like to travel?" I was always curious about where the locals went to get away from the paradise we lived in. Why go to another beach, just to see the beach? Amy did that, but she liked to ride the waves, and apparently—based on some things she keeps telling me and I always ignore—waves are different.

"I used to get in my car and just drive. When I saw somewhere that looked fun, I'd stop for a few days, then take off again." Beth shook her head. "I'm not sure what it is about you two, but you sure get me jawing about myself. I don't think I've talked this much with one customer for years. Let's go find a tree before I tell you about my childhood. Are you sure one of you isn't a shrink?"

Greg walked behind her and Emma trotted next to him. The rows were narrow so only one person could go at a time. Or one person and a dog. Finally, we stopped in a clearing and Beth pointed to a tree. "What about that one?"

I gawked at the tree. It was perfect. Well rounded, just the right height, and exactly the vision I'd had when I decided I wanted a live tree. "How did you do that? This is perfect."

"My job is to put people with the right tree. Something about you two made me come here. I've been saving this tree for someone special, and I guess that's the two of you." Beth grinned. "Is that going to be cash or charge?"

As we drove home with the tree in the back, Greg turned down the music. "I don't know what her overhead is, but it has to be huge if she's charging that much for trees and she can barely make her rent. I guess Esmeralda must have negotiated a price. I'm sure we didn't pay this much last year."

"Don't you think that's some of the spin? You want to buy a tree from her because she needs the money. She's not looking for a handout, just a sale." I squeezed his arm. "You didn't have to pay for the tree. I would have bought it."

"Give me this. After you saying we weren't together, I felt like I needed to show my manliness by buying you an overpriced pine." He turned onto the exit for South Cove. And slowed as he passed Esmeralda's house. She had a Hummer sitting in her driveway. "Esmeralda told me when she left work on Friday that she was booked solid this weekend. Christmas must be a good time for reaching the other side."

"You are such a skeptic." Emma started whining when we pulled into the driveway. "Hold on, girl, I'll let you into the backyard."

As soon as I opened the door, she ran to the side of the driveway and did her business. Then she followed me into the backyard where I shut the gate on her. Going through the back of the house, I came out the front door. "The path is clear."

He put down the tailgate and waved me away as he pulled the tree out of the back. "I can do this. Manly, remember?"

"You're going to pull a muscle." But I stepped back and let him carry the tree into the house through the front door. He lifted it up into the tree stand I'd already set up in front of the window.

"Hold it steady for a minute while I tighten the tree down." Greg's voice came from behind the tree.

I reached into the tree and grabbed the trunk. A guy in a red-checked shirt had sawed off the end of the trunk before he lifted the tree on one shoulder and walked it to the truck. Beth had told us it was so the tree would drink water while it was in the stand. Now, I just had to remember to actually water it. As giddy as I felt about having it in the house, I didn't think that would be a problem. "It fits perfectly. I have the small twinkle lights in different colors, or I could do all white. What do you think?"

"Colors, definitely. I like the way they bounce from one color to the next. You can let go now." He scooted out from under the tree. And then stood behind me and wrapped his arms around me.

"Hey, about what I said back there, about us. I didn't mean we weren't together. I just never know what to say about our relationship."

"Someday you're going to accept the fact that maybe we don't need a label." He squeezed me tight. "I'm perfectly happy just the way we are."

"You are poetic today." But I agreed with him. I just needed to find a way to stop caring about what other people thought. "Too bad you have to leave. This is feeling kind of cozy."

"It's beginning to look a lot like Christmas."

"Earworm," I complained, but I leaned back into him and smiled stupidly at the tree. It was beginning to look like Christmas.

CHAPTER 4

The shop was open on Mondays for a short shift. We closed at four, which meant Aunt Jackie's weekly evening shifts didn't start until Tuesday, giving her a full two-day weekend. As I dragged myself out of bed to go make coffee for my morning commuters, I was beginning to think my aunt had made the schedule change just so she had a full weekend. On the other hand, she deserved some downtime. I decided the shower would wash away my grumpiness.

Once I was at the shop, customers kept me busy until way after eight. When I saw one of my regulars in yoga pants and a sweatshirt instead of her typical power suit, I realized my aunt wasn't the only one with the day off.

"Hey, Candice. You off today?" I paused before making her regular. A lot of times on a day off, people wanted something special. Something with calories, like my favorite, a mocha with whipped cream.

"What gave me away?" She held out her arms, showing off the clothes. "Actually, I'm off until after New Year's. Please make me a double-shot mocha, and I'm going to find a ton of books to take with me on our trip. Robert keeps telling me I can bring my e-reader and save space in my suitcase, but I like the feel of a book. Especially when I'm relaxing."

"Who am I to argue?" I held up a ceramic cup. "You planning on staying a while, or do you want the drink to go?"

"Let's make it to go. I've got a bunch of errands to run before I go home and pack. I'm sorry I'm not going to be here for the party Saturday." Candice set her purse on the counter and pulled out her wallet.

"I'll ring everything up together. I trust you." I started making her drink and then stopped, wide-eyed, as she dropped a hundred-dollar bill in the donation jar we had set up for the animal shelter.

"Oh, I'm not paying you yet." She grinned as I handed her the drink. "I just want to do my part for those poor animals. If I didn't work all the time, we'd consider adopting. But I'd hate to have the dog alone so much."

I waited for her to move toward the racks, then slipped out the bill and put it into the envelope we had in the cash register. Aunt Jackie had made a rule to not leave more than twenty dollars out in cash either in our tip jar or the donation jar. She said it kept people from getting ideas. We'd been lucky so far. Well, South Cove had been lucky. I don't think we've had a robbery for all the time I'd been here. But like my aunt always said, "That's no reason to act stupid."

When Candice came back to the counter, she had ten books, and she handed me a list of ten more. "Could you be a dear and order these for me?"

"Sure. I might have these in next week, but with the holiday, it could delay shipping a few days." I wrote her name on the sheet and tucked it into the book I'd been reading when she came in. "I'll get them ordered this morning."

"I appreciate it." She handed me her credit card and a diamond sparkled on her left hand.

I leaned forward to take in the new ring. It had to be over a carat. "Wow, so is this a celebration trip?"

"Totally. Robert proposed last night. I guess he was planning on doing it once we got to Europe, but he couldn't wait. He was so cute."

"Congratulations." I ran her card and held out the receipt for her to sign. "The ring is lovely."

"It is, isn't it." She signed the slip, then held the card for a minute while she considered the ring. "I'd almost given up on him asking. We've been together for years, but he wanted to focus on his career before he committed to me. It's silly what men think is important. I would have married him if he sold hot dogs at the beach. I'm crazy in love with the guy."

As she walked out, I thought about couples and love and what makes people hold off being happy. Of course, just because someone gets married doesn't ensure they'll be happy. I have empirical proof on that theory since my own marriage didn't work. There were all kinds of reasons we broke up, but I think the main one was we just didn't love each other enough.

I opened my laptop and ordered the books, smiling when I saw that *The Complete Wedding Planner* was one of the books on her list. Candice was going into the next part of this adventure prepared.

By the time Sasha came in to start her shift, I'd been able to curl up and finish one of the young-adult advance reader copies she'd asked me to read. Sasha ran our teen groups as well as a preschool book club every Thursday. The good news is the kids were buying more books and the clubs kept the shop from being empty when the tourist trade was slow. My aunt wanted me to start an early bird book club for women of a certain age. I told her she'd be more effective as the facilitator. So far, that's as far as the idea had gotten.

It's not that I minded running the group, I just didn't want it to take over my reading time.

"It's been pretty slow." I grabbed my jacket. I almost always walked back and forth from the shop to my house. Unless there was a hurricane. And if that happens, I'm not opening the store anyway. So walking works for me. "Call me if you need to. I'm stopping at Diamond Lille's for lunch before I go home."

"Is Greg meeting you?" Sasha started stocking the front coffee bar. Something I could have done if I'd finished the book a few minutes early. I shook off the tiny shred of guilt.

"No. He's got end-of-year inventory to plow through the next two weeks. Esmeralda took this week off for vacation so they're taking turns manning the phones. Even the mayor has had to take a turn."

"I bet that just burned his biscuits." Sasha waved me out of the shop. "Go on. You're off the clock. I'm sure you have a ton of things to get done before Christmas. I brought in my Christmas cards to address, just in case it's slow."

"I'm sure you'll have lots of time to get those done."

Sasha grinned like a kid. "Then you don't mind?"

"I've told you, if we're not busy, you're in charge of your time. As long as the work gets done and the customers are happy, we're golden." I said my goodbyes and headed out of the shop. Josh Thomas was out sweeping the sidewalk. "Morning, Josh."

"What's that supposed to mean?" His response was quick and hard, like a snakebite.

I paused, even though the last thing I wanted was to pick a fight with my neighbor and the only antique dealer in town. Why was he so touchy? The world may never know. "It's a term of greeting. Used between people who know each other or with total strangers who want to be friendly. Do you need me to define the word *friendly* as well?"

"You don't have to be snarky. You don't talk to me much nowadays. Especially since your aunt and I broke up." His eyes misted with tears for a hot second. Then they were gone, as if the emotion had never been there.

"You're right. But honestly, Josh, I was just saying good morning." I looked at the bench that the city had put outside his shop. It had been bare wood, but Kyle, Josh's assistant, had painted the bench a shiny black with green vines and flowers sprinkled over it. The piece was amazing. "Kyle does really good work. You should have him do some things like this for the store."

"I hardly think that craft items would have a place in my antique store." He studied the bench. "Although it is beautifully painted."

"You could sell them as decorative pieces to go along with the antiques. Have Kyle make up some samples for you to look at." I knew Kyle was dying to talk to Josh about this because we'd chatted one day when he was painting the bench. "I'm buying some wooden chairs and a table for the kids' section of the bookstore and he's going to do something around a fairy-tale theme."

"I'll have to talk with him." Josh stared into the window of his shop, probably visualizing how a few decorative pieces would change the look. "People do like that kind of thing."

"They do." I glanced at my watch like I had a real appointment rather than just being starved for lunch. "Oops, I've got to run. Hope to see you at the Christmas party on Saturday."

"I've got my own shop to run, Miss Gardner." He nodded and turned back to his sweeping.

My phone rang as I was walking into Lille's. "Hey, Greg, what's going on?"

"I was hoping to catch you at the shop. Where are you? At home?"

I stepped back outside and sat on one of the benches. "Actually, no. I stopped at Lille's for lunch. Want to join me?"

"I'll be there in ten minutes." He hung up.

I tucked my phone back in my purse and decided to wait outside for him. It was a beautiful day. The sun was shining and there was no wind. If I didn't know Christmas was coming up next week, I would have said it was fall or spring. That's the thing about California, the weather was typically decent. At least I didn't have to worry about scraping my windows or shoveling snow.

"But snow is the best part of Christmas." The voice came from my left, and I turned toward a man dressed in an old-fashioned suit with a red shirt.

It was the guy from the shelter. Had I said that last part aloud? I guess so. "I love the California Christmas. Snow is overrated. Do you live around here?"

"I have a place north of here, but I'm down on a work trip." He nodded to the diner. "Is the food good here?"

"It's the best. Tiny, the cook, he's got a magical way with ingredients." Lille should pay me for the recommendation.

"Magical, you say. Well, I guess I need to check this out." He nodded toward me. "Have a nice day, Jill."

Now, I know I didn't tell him my name. I reached up to see if I had worn the necklace that had my name on it, but no, it wasn't that. I stood and was about to follow him into the restaurant when I heard my name being called.

Greg hurried over to me and gave me a kiss. "You didn't have to wait outside."

"It was a pretty day. Then this guy comes up and he calls me by my name." I tried to peer into the dining room. "He was at the shelter Saturday."

"Ellen probably told him all our names." He took my arm in his. "But if you want me to beat him up, I'll be the macho boyfriend."

"Yeah, that would go over well. A cop beating up an old man." I leaned my head into his arm. "I'm just glad you're here. I'm probably making too much out of this. Ellen probably did tell him my name."

As we walked into the dining room, I glanced around the nearly empty room. The man wasn't here. Maybe he'd gone to the restroom. I paused by the hostess station where Lille scowled at me. "Where's the old man who just came in here?"

"Who are you talking about? Harrold? It's not very nice to point out someone's age." Lille glared at me.

"No, not Harrold. This guy was in a suit, with a red shirt?"

"Look, no one has come in for the last ten minutes. Are you here to eat or argue with me?" She held up two menus like a shield of a knight who was going into battle.

Greg stepped between the two of us. "Two for lunch, please."

He took my arm, and when I started to say something, squeezed it. After we were seated and Lille was back at the hostess station, I glared at him. "What was that?"

"As you and I both know, our diner owner has a habit of kicking out people who make trouble. You, my dear, were making trouble. I could see it on Lille's face. She thought you were messing with her." He studied the menu.

"Greg, I'm telling you that guy came into the restaurant right before you got here." I studied the occupied tables around us. "And now he's gone. Poof, he's vanished."

"People don't vanish, Jill. What book are you reading now?" He set the menu down. "Maybe you need to cut back on the horror genre."

Carrie came up to the table with two iced teas. "Uh, oh. What are you two fighting about? No one's died recently, so it can't be Jill's investigation habit."

"We're not fighting." Greg's calm tone seemed to ease Carrie's concerns. "I'm going with the hot turkey sandwich. What about you, Jill?"

"Turkey club. But can I get mashed potatoes instead of fries?"

After Carrie left, I scanned the room again.

Greg put his hand over mine. "You're certain this guy came inside? Maybe he just went into the foyer, then snuck out when you weren't looking? Who is he?"

"I don't know. But he's getting under my skin." I shook my shoulders. "Anyway, I'm done thinking about him. I'm glad you could do lunch."

"I wanted to show you something." Greg opened the backpack I hadn't noticed him carrying in. Some investigator I was, but I have to admit, I was distracted by the old man.

He set a journal, an old envelope, and a ring box, the type you got when you bought from a real jewelry store, down on the table between us. "This is what was in the safe-deposit box. Baby's owner's name is Thomas Raleigh. I've already sent that over to the Bakerstown guys to run through their systems. But it looks like he's been off the grid for a while. The bank manager said the guy came in once a year, paid for his box and spent some time with the contents."

I held a hand over the envelope. "May I?"

"Of course." He sipped his iced tea as I picked up the fragile paper. "There was one more thing in the box."

I was opening the envelope and pulling out a letter. Absently, I asked, "What else was in the box?"

He touched my hand and I looked up at him.

"Fifty-eight thousand dollars."

CHAPTER 5

Sasha set the letter down and grabbed a tissue. "That is the sweetest thing I've ever read."

She'd come into the shop this morning, even though Toby was working the midday shift, to make sure all the prep work was done for the party. At least that had been her story. And I was glad to pay her the hours, but my gut said she was still hoping that the good-looking barista slash South Cove deputy would look her way again. They'd had one date this summer, before Toby's relationship with another woman had taken off. I had to give it to her, she'd taken the news well. But I could still see the hope in her eyes when she looked at him.

Men. They make our lives wonderful and miserable at the same time. The letter and journal were a prime example. "It gets worse. The journal talks about a house he'd been planning on buying so they could start a family. He'd get the money to buy, and the price would go up, or it would sell. Finally, he ran into a brick wall as the current owner has lived there for over twenty years."

"And he wouldn't ask her to marry him until he had made his way." Sasha shook her head. "Men are hard to understand. They don't get that when you go into a relationship, it's the two of you—it's not just his job to make it work."

"It's an old-fashioned concept, that's for sure." I picked up the letter again. Or actually, a copy of the letter. Greg had followed me to the shop yesterday after lunch, watched me copy the letter and the journal, then left to take the items back to the station for safekeeping. It wasn't often he asked for my opinion on a case, so when he did, I went in full force. Even if it meant doing a little secretarial work. "I've worked since I got out of college. In or out of a relationship, I had money coming in. My aunt always worked, even when she was married to Uncle Ted. But my mom, she felt like she had to depend on her man to make the money. Which sometimes didn't work out so well."

"I guess I'm just a bit of a control freak. I've been almost out-on-the-street poor and I didn't like it. Giving up that power to anyone, including someone I loved, it would be hard." Sasha glanced at the door for the third time that I'd noticed. "Anyway, who do you think this Lizzie is?"

"I'm not sure. We're probably looking for an Elizabeth, but Greg says the guy was at least in his late sixties, so maybe she's already passed on to greener pastures." I pulled out a notebook. "Do you want to help me brainstorm this?"

"I'd love to. If there isn't anything you need me to do for the shop. I am on your dime, so to speak." Sasha grinned, and I saw the determined woman who had blossomed right under our noses.

"You are working. You're keeping me in check. Greg might say that's a full-time job, all on its own." I nodded to the coffee bar. "If you want to do something while we work on this, would you pour me some more coffee? I've got to make cookies tonight and I need the boost."

"Sure." Sasha headed to the coffee bar and poured two cups, bringing them back over to the table. Then, instead of sitting down, she went back to the counter and grabbed two chocolate chip cookies. "We need sugar to get the brain working harder."

"Well played." I bit into the cookie. I started writing down things on the sheet. "So we know his name. He was homeless at the time of death. I wonder where he lived before that?"

"Greg can probably run background now that he knows his name." Sasha nodded to the sheet. "You should ask him if he's done that."

"Good idea, but I think he can only see arrests and things." I tapped the pen on the paper. "But maybe Ms. Google can help us out."

Sasha giggled as I opened my laptop and keyed in Thomas's name and South Cove, California. When a list of sites appeared, I leaned forward, encouraged by the search engine results. Except, they weren't about our Thomas Raleigh. "That was a bust."

Sasha scrolled down the list. "Not so fast. There was a Thomas Raleigh interviewed at the Veterans Center in Bakerstown a few years ago." She clicked and scanned the article. "He was on the streets for at least five years? That's really sad."

I leaned over and looked at the picture. All you could see was the guy's rumpled clothes and his arms as he held a small dog up to the camera. The dog was baring his teeth. Apparently, he didn't like the reporter or the camera. "That's Baby. This is definitely our Thomas. When was that article?" Sasha read off the date and all of the people who were named in the article. I wrote them all down on the paper. My phone rang as I was finishing. "Hello?"

"Where are you? I've been playing ball with Emma for ten minutes waiting for you to get home." Greg's baritone echoed through the speaker.

I glanced up at the clock. "Still at work. Toby hasn't shown up yet."

Sasha shook her head. "I'm here. I'll cover until Toby gets here and then I'll take off since the party stuff is in hand."

"That sounds like a plan," Greg said.

I picked up the phone and took it off speaker. "Hold on a second, will you?"

Sasha shrugged. "What? I'm here, I'm on the clock. I told you to make use of me."

"Okay, but I don't want to hear that Toby talked you into covering his shift so he could have the day off." I closed the notebook and stuffed it and the laptop into my tote. "I'll talk to you tomorrow at the cookie exchange?"

"Most definitely. Granny and Olivia are making up dough now. And as soon as I get home, we'll be decorating. I may have to make ten dozen just to get enough good ones to bring. Olivia likes decorating, she's just not very good at it." Sasha nodded to the couple who'd just walked into the shop. "You go have fun. I think it's cute Greg's helping you bake."

"You and everyone else." I slipped my tote over my shoulder. "Remember, don't work late."

"I promise. Toby Killian isn't going to woo this girl into working any longer than she has to." A wicked smile came over her face. "At least not today."

I power walked home, but it still took me a good ten minutes to get there. Luckily, Greg kept me company on the phone as I walked, telling me all about his day. The one thing he didn't mention was doing any investigating on Thomas. I decided to let it pass until I got home. Then I'd grill him for what he'd found out. In the most gentle and loving way, that is.

Greg and Emma were still in the backyard when I arrived home. He had a key, but typically he waited outside on one of the porches for me to get home. Today, he must have used his key to let Emma out. Sometimes, I found my fridge had been filled with groceries and drinks when I got home. He may not be making himself at home like I'd expected, but he was taking care of me and my dog.

I hung up on him as I walked around the house. "Hey, stranger. Ready for some wicked baking?"

"Making Christmas cookies isn't wicked. It's the opposite." He kissed me and threw Emma's ball one more time. "Have you decided what we're making?"

I nodded, watching my dog fly after the tennis ball. She could run hard when she wanted to. We'd missed our run today as I didn't get out of bed early enough to run *and* take a shower. I chose the shower. "Russian tea cakes. My mother used to make them every Christmas. I'd get powdered sugar all over, but I loved them. I never could sneak one, though. Somehow she always knew."

"Maybe it was the powdered sugar?" Greg held the screen door open as I unlocked the door.

"Probably." I grinned. "Did you eat lunch? I could do some grilled hamburgers if you're hungry."

"I'm starving. I was going to stop at Lille's and bring some chicken, but I forgot and came straight here. Do you want me to go back?"

I shook my head. "No need, we can cook something. Let's just start getting things out that we're going to use. I have the recipe over there."

As we looked for the ingredients, Emma ran out of the kitchen and into the living room. The front door opened, and my aunt called out, "You two better be decent. I don't think my heart could take the shock."

Harrold's deep laugh followed my aunt's announcement. As they came into the kitchen, I smelled the fried chicken before he held up the bags. "We come bearing food. So we can make more food and take it other places and say, we come bearing food."

"And that is the paradox of life. We eat to have the strength to make food so we can eat." Greg took one of the bags and set it on the table. Then he slapped Harrold on the back. "Thanks for bringing the grub. It's nice to see you."

"And you as well." Harrold set the second bag on the table, then stepped over and kissed me on the cheek. "Thanks for inviting us over for this holiday tradition. My late wife and I used to make sugar cookies every Christmas. She loved decorating them."

"No problem." I glanced at Greg, who grinned. I gave Harrold a quick hug. "Sasha and Olivia are bringing those. We're making Russian tea cakes."

"Those are lovely too." He stepped next to my aunt and started taking out the food.

Aunt Jackie smiled up at him. It was a look I'd rarely seen on her face since my uncle had died years ago. She looked happy. Then she saw me watching her and her eyes narrowed. "I've arranged for Toby to cover the last part of my shift tomorrow so I can attend this party with you. Now, why don't you get us some plates and utensils. Greg, pour some iced tea. We need to get to eating before this chicken gets cold."

Following Aunt Jackie's instructions, we were sitting down to lunch in less than five minutes. I glanced at Greg. "Did you learn more about Thomas today?"

"A little, but not much. He was never arrested or charged with anything." Greg picked up a chicken leg. "I guess he kept himself out of trouble."

"Who's Thomas?" Aunt Jackie cut a slice of the chicken breast on her plate with a fork and knife. The rest of us were using our fingers.

I explained about finding the key at the animal shelter and then Greg opening the safe-deposit box and what he'd found.

"Thomas? Thomas Raleigh?" Harrold stared at us. "He's dead?"

"Wait, did you know him?" Greg wiped his hands with a paper napkin.

"Sure. He used to come into the shop, looking for work. He helped me with a lot of the miniature South Cove train display. I'd wondered why I hadn't seen him lately." Harrold laid down his fork and took a sip of tea. "The guy was intelligent, and once you got him talking, you couldn't get him to shut up. I always took him into Lille's for a meal on days he worked for me. Just to make sure he was eating enough."

"I'm so sorry for your loss. Are you all right?" Aunt Jackie covered Harrold's hand with her own.

He smiled at her, which made my heart squeeze just a bit. The smile was filled with such emotion.

"Yes, Jackie. This isn't about me. Thomas was a good man." Harrold leaned back in his chair. "Then that dog in the pound was Baby? I thought he looked familiar, but I never thought Thomas would be gone."

"So did he tell you who Lizzie was?"

Harrold smiled at her. "She was the love of his life. He was trying so hard to fix everything so she'd come back. He was a little obsessed by the idea. I don't think he knew if she was still alive or even in the area anymore."

"His journal talked about how they'd planned on buying a house near the beach just outside Bakerstown. But he'd lost touch with her when he was in the army and when he came home, the house had already sold." I looked over at Greg. "That was what the money was for, to buy the house when he got back home."

"He was devastated. I guess her folks moved up to someplace in Oregon and he tried to send letters, but they were all returned as the forwarding address had expired." Harrold shook his head. "Even the last time I saw him, which must have been forty years after he'd gotten back—it was clear he never gave up."

Aunt Jackie started cleaning up the plates from the table. "Such a sad end to a life. Things that are meant to be, happen, but only if you're open to them. Maybe he could have had a full life filled with love and family if he'd just opened his heart to someone else."

Harrold pulled her close to his chair and hugged her. "Thomas wasn't as lucky as we've been."

The air in the room seemed to stop as I watched my aunt and her new boyfriend. Harrold was good for her. She seemed so happy now. They were meant for each other. But it got me wondering. Aunt Jackie had been meant for my uncle, too. And from what I knew, Harrold was happy with his first wife. Maybe there was more than just one soul mate for each of us. We just had to find the next.

Greg broke the tension in the room. "Let's get baking cookies. Do you want me to turn on the Christmas station?"

One of our radio stations played Christmas carols from the first of November to New Year's Day. It was a solid stream of "Jingle Bells" and other carols sung by a string of different artists, including the barking dogs.

Harrold pulled a few CDs from his jacket pocket. "I've got something better. Mannheim Steamroller. I picked these up last week when Jackie and I attended their concert in the city."

"Perfect." Greg reached out his hand for the CDs. "Come and see the new speaker setup I just installed in the house. We have speakers all through the downstairs and even out on the back porch."

"I'd like to see that." Harrold stood and followed Greg out of the kitchen and toward my study where we'd set up the master system.

"And we're left with the dishes." I finished cleaning off the table, shoving the paper plates and empty containers into a trash bag. "Anything else need to go in here? I'm going to take this right out to the outdoor trash can so Emma doesn't get any ideas about the leftover bones. Of course, that doesn't stop the raccoons from getting them."

Aunt Jackie handed me a bag. "I put the leftover coleslaw and chicken into new containers and they are in your fridge. You should have enough for dinner."

"If we want to eat after making cookies all day. You know we'll have to sample a few."

She smiled. "You always were impatient when it was cookie day."

"They're better when they are warm." I opened the back door. "I'll be right back."

"Jill," my aunt called after me, making me pause. "Thanks for inviting us to share this with you. I like feeling like a family again."

I smiled as I left the house. We'd always been family, but I knew what she was saying. For a lot of years, celebrating the holidays just brought on memories of a past we couldn't recreate. This year, with the addition of friends and loved ones, it felt like the holidays again. Not just a day where we grabbed dinner together and tried making small talk.

Of course, I hadn't invited Aunt Jackie and Harrold to our cookie baking party. But I was glad that Greg had been smarter than me and knew what both Aunt Jackie and I needed before we did. He was a really good boyfriend.

Emma stood at the gate, watching me come back from the trash cans I kept by the side of the garage. I held up my empty hands. "Nothing for you today. Maybe you'll be able to sweet-talk Aunt Jackie out of a treat later."

Just to be sure, she sniffed both hands when I came into the yard, then sulked off to lay in the grass under a tree where she had a few of her toys hidden. We called it Emma's tree house.

"Okay, then, sulk. Just let me know when you want inside." Having Emma outside in the yard while the four of us were busy in the kitchen wasn't that bad of an idea. The golden retriever was gentle with my aunt and Harrold, but she was still large.

I looked back at her. She had her head between her front paws, but instead of watching me, she appeared to be asleep. The dog knew she had time before it was just the two or three of us. And she was patiently waiting.

I wondered if Thomas's Lizzie was patiently waiting for a prince who would never come and rescue her, or if like all modern princesses, she had rescued herself. Tonight, I'd finish reading Thomas's journal and find out if there were any other clues to who this Lizzie was and where in Oregon she could be found.

But today, it was time to make cookies. I walked back into the kitchen where Harrold, Aunt Jackie and Greg were all gathered around the cookbook I'd pulled out for the recipe. Greg smiled at me and waved me over to join the group. The family.

CHAPTER 6

The conference room at city hall was filled with women and smelled like cookies. Christmas carols softly played from a Bluetooth speaker in the corner. And all around the room were tables with cookies. Lots of cookies. I'd met Aunt Jackie at the store. Toby had volunteered to take the end of her late shift. Once he'd arrived, she'd spent more than ten minutes going over the closing procedures. In detail. So instead of arriving promptly at seven, we were fifteen minutes late.

Amy waved us inside. "There you are. You're the last to arrive. Go set up your samples and your bags at the end of the table. Then you can mingle with the others. We have coffee and punch over at the end of the room. Thanks for supplying the coffee, by the way."

"Not a problem. You did place that sign I provided, right?" Aunt Jackie slipped her jacket off and hung it on the coatrack. She kissed Amy on the check. "Oh, there's Mary. I need to talk to her."

As she disappeared through the crowd of women, I shook my head. "She's always marketing. What can you do?"

"I just appreciate the coffee. I didn't want to just serve whatever I could find at the store." She took one of the bags I held and walked with me to our spot on the table.

"Thanks for putting this together. Although I have no idea what I'm going to do with seven dozen cookies." I put the bags on the table and Amy set out the sample dozen. "It looks like everyone's having a good time."

"For my first Christmas cookie exchange, I think I did a good job." She waved at Sasha, who was walking toward us, a dancing Olivia by her side. She knelt to be on Olivia's level. "Hey, beautiful. What's Santa bringing you for Christmas?"

"Santa only brings toys to good little girls," Olivia said, grinning.

"That's right. Have you been good?" Amy picked a cookie crumb off the red velvet dress the little girl wore.

Olivia nodded and took another bite of cookie. "I've been very, very good."

"She thinks so." Sasha laughed. "I hear you had a lot of help to bake your cookies yesterday. Jackie showed me a picture of your tree. It's lovely."

"I'm really happy we got a real tree. It just makes Christmas, you know?" I handed Olivia another cookie.

"She's going to be on a sugar high for days after this." Sasha watched her daughter take a bite of the tea cake and laughed when her eyes lit up. "I think she likes them."

"Sugar, butter, pecans—what's not to like? She has good taste." I caught Olivia's attention. "Are you coming to the bookstore Saturday to see Santa?"

She jumped several times, her eyes brightening. "And puppies."

"You like puppies?"

Olivia nodded. "But we can't have one until we have our own house. Mama says we will soon as we can."

"That sounds smart." Amy glanced over toward the end of the room. "I better get this thing started."

Sasha watched as Amy walked away toward the middle of the room. "She's in her element here."

"She does like throwing a party." Olivia took off to look at the Christmas tree. Greg had gone back to the tree lot and not only gotten a real tree for the station, but also one for the conference room, as he knew Amy was using it for her party. "I learned something new about Thomas yesterday."

"Really?" Sasha quickly switched her gaze from watching her daughter to my face, then back.

"He was in the army. I read the entire journal and it was written like he was talking to her. He'd been sent out on a long patrol and had missed mail for several weeks. When he got back, there was a letter saying she'd moved, but the address she gave him was a PO box. Then the letters stopped coming."

"She stopped writing?" Sasha waved at her daughter, who was standing by the tree, waving at her.

"I think she thought *he* stopped writing. Soon, his letters came back as undeliverable. He blamed her parents." I laughed watching as Olivia picked up one present after another and shook them.

"They probably thought she was too young. You know how protective parents can be."

"True. But I found out something else. Harrold knew Thomas." I pointed to Olivia, who was now picking one cookie from each plate and switching them to a new plate.

"I better rein her in. I'll come in early for my shift tomorrow and you can tell me the rest of the story. It's like watching a romantic movie, although we know this one has a sad ending." She scurried over toward her daughter. "Olivia Ann Smith. You stop that right now."

"Usually, I don't think children should be allowed at these things." My aunt had rejoined me after Sasha left. "Of course, Olivia is a very curious child. It shows her intelligence."

Amy started talking just in time so I didn't have to answer my aunt. Sometimes, I think she liked Olivia more than the rest of us.

We spent the rest of the evening picking out cookie bags to take home and mixing with friends. Christmas wasn't turning out half bad after all.

* * * *

The next morning, I had seven dozen cookies sitting on my kitchen table, staring at me. Plus I still had three dozen of the Russian tea cakes from our baking session. I bundled most of the cookie bags into a tote bag. I had a plan for them.

First stop, after working my shift at the coffee shop, was the funeral home to see Doc Ames. I'd have to drive into Bakerstown, so I left the cookies in the bag and put them up in the plate cupboard where Emma couldn't reach them. Doc probably wouldn't be able to tell me much about how Thomas had died, but the coroner slash funeral director had lived in Bakerstown all his life. Maybe he knew some of the Thomas and Lizzie story.

I got to the shop but didn't have a customer all morning. Thursday morning was typically slow, but the fact it was less than a week away from Christmas had dried up the commuter traffic. Either people weren't working today or they were trying to get in early to clean up work so they could take a Christmas holiday. Either way, I didn't mind. A slow customer day meant more reading for me. And I took advantage of the time.

By the time Sasha arrived, I'd finished the mystery and was working on a young adult book set during New Year's that her book club was discussing in January. She stopped at the coffee bar to grab a cup, then plopped down in the chair across from me. "How do you like it?"

"I love it. Such a great story. You're really good at picking books." I slipped a bookmark into the book and set it on the table next to the mystery. I tapped the other book. "This one's excellent too."

She picked it up. "Mind if I take this? I need something a little darker after I read one of Olivia's books over and over at bedtime. You can only take so much of happy monsters before you want to scream. I mean really, where are the bad monsters?"

"In the adult books." I went to refill my coffee. "So what else did you want to know about Thomas?"

She listed off what she did know and I flipped open my notebook, adding to each point I had in my notes. "There isn't much more to say. Except, I'm going to deliver cookies to a couple of places today. Maybe I'll find out more."

"Someone's going to have a very merry Christmas if you and Greg figure out where the money is supposed to go." Sasha sighed as she sipped her coffee. "That much money would be enough to put a down payment on a house. Prices are crazy here on the coast. That's why I'm not even looking until I have my degree. Who knows where Olivia and I will wind up. I don't want to have to worry about a house I need to sell."

"I know I'm not going to get my Christmas wish, but I kind of hope you find some rich guy, marry him, and stay around. I'd miss talking to you if you move across the country."

"My future mantra is 'show me the money.' But honestly, I'd rather work for it myself than be given it by some guy. And if I do marry well, as my gran says, I'll be sure to tuck some money away into a rainy day fund. Just in case. Like I said, you never know about men."

"Sounds like a smart plan." I glanced at the clock. "Well, if I'm going to get to Bakerstown and see Doc Ames before he closes for his afternoon nap, I better get going. Are you working tomorrow?"

"Yeah. Toby had a shift with Greg come up so he asked me to cover his slot." She held up her hand, warding off what she thought I was going to say. "I need the hours. If he wants to give them to me, I'm not going to complain. No matter the reason behind why he can't work."

"It's your life." I smiled to soften the words. "I just don't want to see you getting hurt."

"I'm a big girl. I know Toby's Kryptonite for me. I just need to keep our relationship at the friends and coworkers level. Dating someone in South Cove would be too hard. How do you break up with someone you see every day?"

Sasha's question hung with me all the way to Bakerstown. As soon as I'd arrived at the house after leaving work, I'd moved the cookies from their hiding place out of Emma's reach to the car. Then I'd grabbed the leash and my dog. The day was turning out to be cool and beautiful, so since I wouldn't be at either of my stops long, I'd decided to take Emma with me on the road. She sat in the front, glancing back at the rear of the vehicle where I'd stored the cookies. I had a police-type wire enclosure that either kept her in or out of the back of the vehicle, depending on my mood. Today, I wanted her front and center with me. Mostly so I could talk out my different theories with her. She never interrupted and rarely told me I was stupid for even thinking that way. Of course, Greg never said stupid either, but he did get this sad expression when he found out I was investigating something he'd told me to stay out of.

I really needed to get a new hobby.

I pulled into the empty parking lot and rolled Emma's window down. I went into the back and got one of the premixed bags of cookies I'd made on Wednesday night. Then I grabbed a second. Doc Ames lived alone and from what I knew didn't have many friends. I suppose that being the doctor of the dead kept people from bonding, even if the guy was one of the sweetest men in Bakerstown. I locked the doors and went to the home. Wandering through the empty building, I got the creeps.

Luckily, Doc Ames must have heard me come in, as he popped out of a doorway and asked, "Can I help you?" He blinked in the dim light. "Oh, Jill, I didn't realize it was you. Is this a personal or professional visit?"

"Kind of both. I brought cookies." I followed him back into his office and set my tote on one of the two visitor chairs. "And I wanted to pick your brain a little. I wanted to find out what you knew about Thomas Raleigh."

"Oh, Thomas. I can't believe I didn't recognize him when I did the autopsy. You know we went to school together here at Bakerstown High." He poured two cups of coffee and slid one over to me. "He played football and was in the concert band. Trumpet, if I remember."

I knew this was the right place to come. Doc Ames knew everyone in the area. "Was he dating anyone?"

"Of course. He and Lizzie were joined at the hip as soon as she showed up her freshman year. He was a junior so her folks weren't too happy about his attention. But they stayed together, no matter what the problems. When he went off to the army, she…" Doc Ames bit into a cookie, frowning a little. "I think she must have moved away. I was away at college, but you hear things, especially when you come back. And her folks moved her to Washington or Idaho."

"Maybe Oregon?" I prompted the memory.

He nodded. "That was it. A little town up in the mountains. And that's the last I heard about Lizzie. Thomas came home the year I went to medical school. I hear he tried to find her, but there wasn't any trace. I guess her parents won that war after all."

He sipped his coffee and ate another cookie. "I'm ashamed to admit I didn't follow up with Thomas after I got back. I'd just gotten married and my father was ready for me to take over, so my days and nights were filled with either my family or the dead. Then I was talked into taking on the job of county coroner, and the years flew by."

"You can't blame yourself." I sipped my coffee. "Greg was saying he died of natural causes."

"Oh, he did. But maybe if I'd been a better friend, he wouldn't have wound up homeless and on the streets for the last few years of his life." He shook his head at the memory. "Regrets are just a way of not dealing with today. You can't change the past, now, can you?"

"No, you can't."

We sat in silence as we finished our coffee. Then I stood. "Thanks for talking to me. I didn't mean to make you sad."

"I'm not sad, and you didn't make me feel bad. I'm just thinking about the past. And when I get down that trail, sometimes it's hard to pull myself out. I'm planning on coming down for your party on Saturday. I've decided I need to find a senior cat who's as grumpy and hard to get along with as I am. That way, we'll suit each other just fine."

I hurried out to the car. Emma sat on the seat, watching the door to the funeral home. When I came out, she barked at me.

"I'm coming. Sorry, I needed to talk to Doc Ames for a bit." Before I got into the car, I clipped on her leash and led her to the sidewalk and the strip of grass between the parking lot and the road. "Do your business."

Emma found a tree and watered it, then came back to my side. I always carried water and a bowl in the car so I got it out and poured her a drink. When I figured she was satisfied, we loaded up and got ready to go to our next stop.

The Veterans Center was in its own building just down the street from the mortuary. I guess they got a good deal on the property since most people don't want to live down the street from the place where they take care of the dead.

I checked Emma's window, grabbed the rest of the cookies, then locked up the doors. "You be good. I'll be right back out and we'll go for a run on the beach when we get home."

This time, I could see the grin on her face. Dogs. Who says they can't understand what we say?

I walked up the few steps, then into the open lobby area. People sat around what looked like an oversize living room. A few men played cards at a table. In the back, I could see a dining room set up and the room smelled like pasta and garlic bread. I started to move toward a large desk where a man sat, but Beth from the Christmas tree lot stopped me. She had her jacket on and a purse over her shoulder. Apparently, she was leaving.

"Hey, how'd the tree work out for you?" Beth smiled and shrugged. "Sorry, I don't remember your name, but that tree was gorgeous. And your man came back on Monday and bought two more. I adore repeat customers. I hope to see you next year."

"Definitely. The tree is beautiful." I glanced around the room. "Are you visiting someone?"

She shook her head. "Volunteering. I come in a few times a week and help with lunch. It's the least I can do for people who have given so much for this country."

"That's nice."

"Anyway, I've got to get back to the lot. You leave those boys alone long enough, they'll start playing Paul Bunyan and throwing axes at each other." She shook her head. "Don't laugh, it's happened."

"Thanks again for the tree," I called out as she took off for the door.

When I turned back around, the guy at the desk was watching me. "Let me guess, cookie exchange?"

"Does my desperation show on my face?" I walked over and dropped the tote bag filled with cookies. "Can I donate them? The exchange was just on Wednesday. They should be fresh."

"Of course. The guys love a little homemade now and then. A lot of these guys have either lost their spouse or never remarried after an early divorce." He leaned into the tote and took out one of the bags of the Russian tea cakes. "I love these. My mom used to make them."

"Thank you for taking the cookies." I glanced around and wondered if I should press my luck. "Can I ask you a question?"

"Shoot." He opened the bag and took a big whiff of the vanilla. "These may not make it back to the guys to share."

I smiled as he popped a whole cookie into his mouth. "I've been doing some research on someone who was a veteran. I wondered if he'd ever come in the center."

"You're talking about Thomas, aren't you?" When he saw the shock on my face, he laughed. "Don't think I'm a mind reader or nothing. It's just a small town. People talk, especially when one of us dies."

CHAPTER 7

"Do you mind?" I nodded to a chair near the desk.

He stood and moved it toward me. "Sorry, I should have offered you a seat. Anyway, what do you want to know about Thomas?"

I waited for him to return to his own chair. I was looking farther into the past, but maybe talking to this guy who had known him recently would give me some clues. "How often did he come in here?"

"When I first came on, about ten years ago—man, I can't believe I've been here ten years." He shook his head. "Anyway, he was here when I got here. He'd come in most days, scan the paper and make some calls. If he got a day job, he'd miss a few days, then he'd be back. The guy was driven, you know?"

"Did you ever talk to him about his high school sweetheart?"

He laughed and took another cookie. "Dude, that's all Thomas wanted to talk about. It's a sad story. He went into the army and her folks moved her away. He's been, I mean, was, looking for Lizzie all his life. Anytime he'd have enough in his pocket for a train ticket, he'd ride up to Oregon and try to find her. Now that's love."

"But lately?" When I saw the confused look, I repeated the man's words. "You said when you first got here, that is what he was doing. What was his behavior the last few months?"

"He'd only show up for meals, then take off. He always had that dog with him." A sad smile creased his face. "He'd talk more to the dog than to anyone here. After a while, we just let him be."

This was not what I wanted to hear. Maybe I'd never find out what happened to Thomas and Lizzie. Some stories didn't end with a bang; instead, they fizzled out. Emma was waiting in the car and I needed to go. I stood and reached into my bag. I scribbled on the back. "Thank you for your time. I'm Jill Gardner. I run the coffeehouse in South Cove. If you're ever in town, stop by, give that to whoever is the barista and I'll buy you a drink."

"That's nice of you." He pocketed the card. "I'm Ben Woodsmen. And I better get back to decorating the tree before Christmas comes and goes."

I turned toward his nod. A fresh tree sat in the corner, recently delivered. "Did that come from Beth at Lumberjack Phil's Christmas Pines?"

"She's such a wonderful lady. She donates a tree every year. And she's in here a lot to help cook, although the last few weeks she's been too busy with the lot to spend much time here. I noticed you two talking on your way in. Did you buy a tree from her?"

Nodding, I realized a connection was starting to form in my head. "Ben, did Thomas bond with anyone or did anyone show him any specific interest?"

"Funny question, but now that I'm thinking about it, Beth was always asking if he'd been in to eat. She worries about some of our older guys since they sometimes think they can drink their calories from a bottle. She always made sure she touched base with Thomas on the days he came in."

"Hey Ben, where's the box with the lights? We have to put those on first." An older man was looking through a large cardboard box on a table near the tree.

"Sorry, I have to go. It was nice talking to you, and thanks for the cookies."

As I left the building, I saw Emma watching for me. Her head was laying on the dashboard like she'd been waiting forever instead of the ten minutes I'd been in the center. The weather was still cool, but soon, it would be too hot to leave her in the car for even that long. We went through our routine as I let her out and gave her water. This time, she didn't drink as much. My mind was on Thomas.

When we got on the road, I called Amy using my car's Bluetooth. When she answered, I asked for a favor. "Could you call your counterpart in Bakerstown and find out who is the owner on record for Lumberjack Phil's Christmas Pines?"

"Something wrong with your tree? I love the ones Greg bought for the station and the conference room. Something about pine screams Christmas."

"No. I just have a theory." I turned into a local drive-in, Buster's Burgers, and Emma leaned her head out of the window, catching all the smells. I needed to delay my exit from Bakerstown until I got the information. "Can you call me right back?"

"Sure. Be back in a few."

Both Emma and I had finished our burgers by the time Amy called back. The dog was eyeing my fries, but she'd had an unfortunate stomach incident the last time I'd fed her fries and I didn't need her messing up my carpet.

"Sorry that took so long. Terri wasn't in the office so I called her cell. She's out Christmas shopping this afternoon, but she'll call me first thing in the morning with the info. Will that work?"

"It will have to." I batted down Emma's paw as she tried to move the fries closer to her seat. "Thanks for doing this. I'll talk to you tomorrow."

"Want to grab lunch?"

I glanced at the clock; it was past one. "Sorry, Emma and I just got hamburgers. Should I go back through the drive-up and get you something?"

"No. I have a salad in the fridge. I just wanted to get out of here for a while. The place is dead. The mayor and Tina took off for two weeks on a cruise of the Caribbean on Monday. So I'm almost caught up on filing. I guess I'll have to read to pass the time."

"Nice work if you can get it," I teased.

"Hey, you shouldn't talk. You read at the shop all the time." We made plans for brunch on Sunday and hung up. I glanced over at Emma, who was still plotting a way to get the rest of the fries. Instead, I bagged them up with the trash and threw it in a trash can near the parking lot. Returning to the car, I could see the question in her eyes. *Why did you throw away such yummy goodness?*

"It's for your own good." I started the engine and headed toward the coastal highway. By the time we got there, Emma had forgotten her disappointment and was hanging her head out the window to grab all the ocean smells.

My investigation was at a dead end until tomorrow. So this afternoon, Emma and I would run the beach.

* * * *

Friday morning the shop was, if possible, even slower than it had been the prior day. I finished off all of Aunt Jackie's party prep list, cleaned the entire front of the shop, and still had time to sit with a mocha and a new book before Sasha came in to replace me.

Just before ten, Amy called. "Did you know, the owner of Lumberjack Phil's Christmas Pines is not a guy named Phil. Funny how that happens."

"So who owns it?"

"A woman named Elizabeth Ann Ries. She's owned it from the beginning. And before you ask, she also owns a house near Big Rock Point off the highway between here and Bakerstown." She read off the address and paused for me to write down the information. "Does this have to do with the secret of Baby's collar?"

"Yes. And before you say it, Greg already knows I'm investigating this. For once, I have his permission."

I glanced at the clock. I could call Sasha in early. But with Olivia to get ready and Sasha probably studying for some class, I didn't want to bother her. Toby was working for Greg this weekend. Aunt Jackie would ask too many questions. And Nick, our summer part-time barista, was on a two-week skiing vacation in Aspen.

Briefly, I entertained the idea of closing until Sasha arrived, but then discarded that as well. I'd just have to wait until my relief showed up before heading out to see if my theory was right. So I went back to reading and ignored the what-ifs running through my brain.

Just before noon, Ellen from the shelter called. "Just checking in to see if we need to do anything before tomorrow."

"I think we're good. We'll set up the dogs that get along in an open pen in the children's section. Santa will be in the dining room. And we'll have a table in front of the bookshelves for the cats."

"Sounds great. Is there a place we can walk the dogs? I know the party is only six hours, but we'll have to rotate them in and out at least a few times."

"We've blocked off the back parking lot so it will be available for your use. You can use the back door for easy access." We had tomorrow's party planned to a tee. Thanks to my aunt and Sasha. They just let me know what's going on and I sign the checks.

"I made up a handout of the joys of adopting, especially senior pets, from the shelter. Hopefully some of our older guys will find homes." She sighed. "Everyone wants puppies."

"I think we'll find a lot of homes tomorrow. And we've already raised a lot of cash for your operating expenses. It's going to be a great day."

Ellen didn't quite share my enthusiasm, but she did seem happy about the money influx. It must be hard to keep a shelter financially solvent. I decided I'd write a check tomorrow from the Miss Emily fund. My friend had left me money when she died, and other than using some of it for a scholarship here and there, I'd been looking for a charity to support. I made a note on tomorrow's schedule to bring in a check.

"I can't believe we're still so slow. Do you think anyone's coming to the party tomorrow?" Sasha arranged a few chairs as she strolled through the dining room.

"I think everyone's coming to the party tomorrow, which is probably *why* we're so slow." I packed my laptop and the book I'd been reading into my tote. "I hate to run out of here, but I need to talk to someone."

"Is this about the mystery of the homeless man and the money?" She slipped off her jacket and pulled back her curly hair into a loose ponytail at her neck. Then she slipped on her CBM apron and washed her hands.

"Maybe. I'll tell you all about it tomorrow, if it pans out. Otherwise, I got nothing." I walked home, and after letting Emma out for a quick second, I grabbed my purse and notebook and jumped into my Jeep.

My first stop was Lumberjack Phil's Christmas Pines. When I finally found a young man who was working, I broke up their wood-chopping contest. "Where's Beth?"

"She called in today. I'm in charge. Can I help you?" He looked to be maybe eighteen and probably still in school.

"No, that's okay. But maybe you should hang out at the shed where customers can find you." As I walked away I heard the mumblings that my suggestion had brought on. *Not my circus, not my monkeys*, I reminded myself.

I drove to the other address Amy had given me. A small cottage sat just off the road. The yard was dormant for the season but she still had flowers blooming in pots near the door. You could see the ocean from the side of the house and I bet the back had a porch or a deck that had at least one chair aimed that way for watching the sun set.

I knocked on the door. Beth opened it and peered out at me with red, swollen eyes. "What are you doing here?"

"Can I come in? I need to ask you a few things."

Beth narrowed her eyes, then her shoulders drooped. "Why the hell not. Do you want coffee?"

"That would be nice." Although I'd probably drank more than my daily allotment at the shop while I was waiting for Sasha. I walked into the small, clean living room and saw a picture of a young black man standing behind a young Beth, holding her tightly and grinning into the camera. I heard her come back behind me.

"You didn't know Tommy was black, did you? Don't worry, I can see it on your face." She motioned to the chair by where she'd set the coffee down. "It's kind of amazing; you're investigating what happened to Thomas and you never even considered he wasn't white."

"No one said anything. And, I guess, this is the first picture I've seen of him." I sat down and sipped the coffee. "That's why your parents were so upset. You are Lizzie, right?"

"I am. And yeah, my folks were worried about what would happen. How hard it would be on both of us if we got married. It was a different time then. I'm not excusing them, but I can understand now." She walked over and picked up the picture. "It was why he went into the service. To prove to them he was dependable and he'd take good care of me. I was just sixteen when he left, but he was the love of my life."

"So you didn't know he lived here." I didn't want to confront her about his being homeless.

"The first time I saw him after that was probably twenty years ago. I'd moved back, bought our dream house, and had started volunteering at the Vet Center. I was trying to find him. To see if he'd come home. I figured he was married and raising a passel of young ones by then." She walked over and picked up the picture, carrying it back to the sofa and setting it on the coffee table. "So when I saw him, I was overcome with emotion. But he didn't recognize me."

"Why?" I looked at the love pouring out of the picture and couldn't understand what she was telling me. These two people were desperately in love.

"I'm not sure. I heard from someone that he was injured in combat. Head trauma. I thought, maybe, if I kept showing up, he'd recognize me. But he just knew me as Beth, the nice woman who let him ramble about his Lizzie. Near the end, I don't think he even knew me as Beth. All he cared about was that dog. And a sixteen-year-old girl he'd left behind and lost."

"I'm so sorry." I sipped my coffee, thinking about how hard that must have been. "My, I mean, Greg King is looking for you. Thomas left you some money and an engagement ring. There's a letter and a journal too. Maybe that might help."

"I could use the money. I wasn't kidding when I said the trees don't keep me in money for the year. But the ring isn't mine. It's for a girl who no longer exists. He made that perfectly clear every time we talked." She leaned back on the couch and let her gaze focus on the ceiling. "Is it crazy that I'm jealous of her? Of the younger me? I held on to the idea of us for so long that when I realized it was never going to happen, it crushed me."

"His dog is at the shelter. Maybe you could take him in?" I'd like to get Baby settled before tomorrow's party. Living here with Beth, they could help each other heal.

"I know, and I can't take that dog in. All it would do is bring back memories of a life we never got to live." She looked around the cottage. "I've been living here for too long. This is our dream that never came to be. I need to find my own dreams."

"Well, if you change your mind, call me." I left my card on the coffee table by my cup. "Baby's really sweet."

She followed me to the door. "Thank you for coming by. I'll give Mr. King a call this afternoon. But I won't be adopting Baby."

I was depressed as I drove home, so I called Amy and related everything that had happened. "I can't believe she's not taking in the dog."

"I can't believe he didn't recognize her. You hear the stories about people finding each other all the time. After twenty years, they'll be at the same shopping mall and run into each other. Love is supposed to work that way." Amy sniffed into the phone.

"Now I have you depressed too." I focused on driving back to South Cove. "I guess his brain got rewired after the accident. He knew he'd loved Lizzie. But Beth wasn't Lizzie, not anymore. Anyway, I'll see you in the morning. Let's hope we get all the dogs and cats new homes. I need a mark in the win category this week."

When I got home, I grabbed a blanket, turned on the sappiest love story I could find, and cried into Emma's fur.

CHAPTER 8

Early Saturday afternoon, the party was in full swing. Santa had a good-size line of kids waiting to talk to him. The dogs and cats were getting along without much barking or hissing. And Ellen was ecstatic, as she'd had five placements in the first hour. Greg came by and stood next to me. He kissed me on the cheek. He'd come over last night after Beth had called him and told him the story.

"This is a good thing you're doing here." He nodded to Doc Ames, who was talking to Ellen while holding Rex, a large gray cat. Apparently, the prior family had named him after a dinosaur. When they moved, they couldn't take the aging feline. Rex leaned into Doc Ames's hand and I could swear I heard the purr all the way over where I stood.

"I know. I'm just sad about Baby." I squared my shoulders. "I tried to talk Aunt Jackie into taking him but she blew me off. I guess if he's still up at the end of the party, he's mine. Emma will just have to deal."

"I think she has room in her heart for another dog. Just don't expect her to share her toys. She can be a little protective of them, even with me." Greg nodded when Ellen waved him over. "It's my turn to take a dog outside. I swear, I'm not this busy at work."

I smiled as he walked away, and felt a hand on my arm. I turned to greet the newcomer, but my smile faded as I recognized her. "Beth, what are you doing here?"

"Thank you for coming by yesterday. I'm afraid I was having a small pity party." She smiled and patted my cheek. "I'm here to do I should have done weeks ago. I'm claiming Thomas's dog. At least we'll have each other."

As she walked to the pen, Baby stood on his hind legs and whined at her. He recognized her. Thomas hadn't been able to, but Baby knew the woman who was walking toward him. Maybe he recognized the love she'd tried to pour into Thomas or just recognized her as someone he'd met in the past, but the dog was ecstatic to see her. And the feeling was mutual. I heard Beth's voice as she picked him up out of the cage. "Hey, Baby, do you want to come home with me?"

The dog barked his answer and I smiled after wiping the tears from my eyes. Baby was going to have a very merry Christmas.

"You did good, Jill. Thanks for making her so happy." Santa stood by me, a cookie in his hand.

"She just had to find her way." I swallowed hard. "I'm just happy that Baby isn't alone anymore."

"Neither of them is alone, now. Thanks to you. And that's the true meaning of the season, being with others." Santa turned and looked at his line. "Time to go back and finish up my list."

I watched him walk back to the chair they'd set up where Sasha could take a picture of each child on Santa's lap.

"You okay?" Greg paused with a wriggling boxer on the leash. The dog knew where they were going and was anxious to get there.

"I'm perfect." I glanced around the crowded Coffee, Books, and More, and realized I was just fine. I was home.

A Pumpkin Spice Killing

A Farm-to-Fork novella

Chapter 1

Angie Turner leaned back in the shotgun seat in one of the two minivans she'd rented for the County Seat's most recent team building session. Hope Anderson, the restaurant's newest line cook, had been in charge of planning the session this quarter and she'd wanted to get the team building started as soon as the vans left the County Seat's parking lot.

"Pull the van into that coffee place and let's get something to drink. My treat." She pointed Ian McNeal, van driver and her boyfriend, to the upcoming coffeehouse. "I'll let Felicia know we're stopping at the drive-thru."

"Your wish." Ian grinned at her, then looked into the back of the van at Hope and Bleak Hubbard. They'd chosen to ride together in the front van with the addition of Dom, Angie's St. Bernard and County Seat mascot. The girls had become fast friends as soon as Bleak had arrived in River Vista. "You two old enough for coffee or should we get you hot chocolate?"

"I've been drinking coffee for years." Bleak tossed her hair back out of her eyes. She'd dropped the goth look, but her hair was still long and black. Now it had a healthy shine to it and Angie noticed she and Hope had matching pedicures with what looked like animals painted on the nails. "Anyway, get me a pumpkin spice latte. It's time to welcome fall."

"Yes, it is." Angie finished texting their stop to Felicia and, looking up from her phone, grinned at the newest member of the restaurant family. Bleak was still in high school, but she'd talked her school counselor into approving this community service trip even though it meant she'd miss three days of school. "I'll have the same. Large, please."

"You mean venti," Hope corrected her. "I'm in for the PSL too."

Ian shook his head. "Okay, three coffee light drinks and a real cup of coffee for me."

"Don't be that way. PSL is amazing." Hope curled her leg up underneath her and reached back to stroke Dom's back. He was back on the third seat sleeping. He lifted his head and gave Hope's hand a quick lick before plopping his head back down on the seat. "Does Dom need some water?"

"I gave him some before we left town and I've got a couple of bottles in that backpack on the floor. He'll let you know if he's thirsty." Angie loved how well Dom fit in with the group. He was as much of a family member as any of her staff.

"Depending on how many more stops I have to make, we should be there in about two hours." Ian glanced at the GPS he'd brought with him.

"Angie, do you think Matt bought that we were going to a knitting retreat?" Hope leaned forward toward the front of the van. "Did you see his face when I handed him the bag with yarn and knitting needles?"

"I thought the mini lesson/project sheet you gave him was awesome. He should be trying to figure out how to hold the needles right now. Nancy said she'd help him on the ride." Angie turned to face Hope. "When you set up a prank, you go all in."

"I can't believe he took us to a haunted prison last fall. It really wasn't fun. Especially after that guard was killed. If we make it through the next four days with no one dying, I'm calling this a success." Hope leaned back in her seat. "Especially when Matt finds out we're helping clean up this veteran's home instead of knitting."

"He's going to whine about that too." Bleak didn't look up from her fashion magazine. "Matt always whines when there's actual work to be done. I'm surprised Estebe hasn't moved him back to dishwasher as much as he complains about things."

"He's just young," Ian said as he pulled up to the speaker at the coffeehouse. "Hey, they have pumpkin bread too. Four slices?"

"Sounds like a plan." Angie opened her planner and started to make notes about the new menu she wanted to propose at the staff meeting they would have in a few days out at the farmhouse before they would pack up for home. She'd told the center's owner that the group would handle food for the center for the time they were there. She and Felicia would see what they needed and check for any specific dietary issues with the residents, then head to the local grocery store to stock the center's shelves.

They'd had to make the quarterly team building event smaller for the last few quarters, but this time, she was going all out. And she'd have time to test some of the recipes she wanted to propose.

Angie took the cups of pumpkin spice latte Ian handed her and passed two back to Hope and Bleak. She was getting into the road trip mood. The team building was going to be an amazing four days. Especially once Matt got over being tricked with the yarn.

By the time they reached River Vista Veteran's home, it was almost eleven. Angie got out of the van and took in the house and surrounding area. It was an old ranch-style home that needed a touch up. According to Hope, the woman who ran it, Mrs. Stewart, had been managing the center for over ten years. The house looked like it hadn't been painted in at least that long. The front yard needed weeding and grass planted. They had their work cut out for them.

Ian stood by her and whistled. "I didn't think it would be this bad. Hopefully the inside is better off, or we'll have to prioritize what we get done this time. I'll get my men's group to come out next month. We'll get this place ready for new residents. Don't worry."

"I didn't say I was worried," Angie responded.

He laughed and pulled her into a hug. "Honey, sometimes your face tells the whole story. It will be fine. I promise."

The other van pulled up and the rest of the crew joined them in front of the house. Matt stepped out and went to stand by Hope. "Wow. This place looks like it needs some work. Are you sure we're at the right place?"

"How's your knitting going?" Hope didn't look at him but Bleak snickered.

He glared at the young women. "This isn't a knitting retreat, is it? We're here to fix this place up."

"He gets it right on the first guess." Hope stepped forward to greet the woman who walked out of the house and onto the rundown porch. "Mrs. Stewart? I'm Hope Anderson and this is the County Seat crew. Angie and Felicia are our fearless leaders."

Angie and Felicia held up their hands.

"Well, isn't this nice. I so appreciate young people taking an interest in the people who served our country so many years ago. We have only two men in residence right now. Randy Owens and Kendrick Trickle. Both men saw the fall of Saigon and have a lot of stories to tell about their time. Randy's not been feeling well recently so he's probably not up to having visitors. It's sad when they're in the last days." Mrs. Stewart waved them forward. "Come on in, I'll show you your rooms."

"This is going to be an amazing few days." Hope took Bleak's hand and they were the first on the porch. Felicia and Angie exchanged a look and followed the crew into the house.

Yes, this was going to be an interesting team building session, Angie thought. She hoped that Bleak and Hope were up to the challenge. Although Angie didn't know why she was worried. Both of the young women came from families where service to others was something expected rather than just a once-a-year thing.

Mrs. Stewart stopped at a room and opened the door. "Girls room here. Boys will be on the other side of the hallway. I've left linens for the beds. I have iced tea and cookies in the parlor and I'll give you the to-do list. Now, don't think you have to get everything done in four days. Choose your projects. I'm sure God will send more helpers to our doorstep soon."

"My dad's men's group is planning a weekend to come up next month to help." Hope pointed toward Ian. "So you'll get to see that guy again. It's okay though, he's cool."

Mrs. Stewart smiled and nodded. "I've been talking to a third group out of River Vista who are coming soon. God really is good. Men, come this way and I'll show you your room."

Inside their room, Hope dropped her bag onto a top bunk. "Bleak, do you want top or bottom. Or you could have that top over there and we could talk?"

"Don't think you two girls are going to be chatting all night. I need my eight hours or I'm a bear. Just ask my kids." Nancy nodded to Angie. "Boss, do you want the single or do you and Felicia want the bottom bunks?"

"We'll take the bottom bunks." Felicia ran over to claim her bed. "This is so much fun. It's like camp."

"I don't know what camp you went to but we were in actual tents." Angie followed her over and motioned Dom to sit on the floor between the two bunks. "Let's get our beds made and stuff situated and then we can get busy. Daylight's wasting."

"Yes, mother," Felicia said behind her.

"I'd hit you with my pillow but I'm afraid it might break apart." Angie stuffed her pillow into a well-worn pillowcase with faded embroidery on the edge. "We may want to buy linens for the residents' rooms as our company Christmas charity."

"Great idea. I'll check it out and see what's needed." Felicia grabbed her phone and made a note.

Angie finished putting her clothes away in a drawer, then grabbed Dom's backpack and started unloading his stuff on top of the dresser. She put his canned food at the back and his bag of treats on top of that. Maybe he wouldn't sniff them out. "It's bad when I pack lighter for me than my dog, isn't it?"

"You spoil him." Felicia stood by the door. "Come on slowpoke. The girls are already heading to the living room for cookies."

Angie and Dom followed Felicia out but as she walked past a room, she heard a noise.

"Carol? Is that you?" A man's voice called out.

Angie glanced in the room and saw an elderly man sitting in a chair near the window looking outside. "Sorry, it's not Carol. My name is Angie Turner and this is my dog, Dom."

"He sure is a big fellow." The man reached out a withered hand and Dom went over to sit where the man could pet him.

Dom seemed to know when his services as a big fuzzy love puppy were needed. And this was one of those times. Angie moved closer so the older man could see her face. There was a metal folding chair near the wall, and she set it up so she could sit down for a minute. "How are you today? We're here to work on the house. I hope we won't be too noisy for you."

"Don't worry about me." The man grinned. "I'm only glad to have someone to talk to besides Carol. She means well, but she has a lot of work to do to keep all of us going. I'm Randy Owens. It's genuinely nice to meet you and Dom."

Angie noticed he hadn't taken his hand off the large dog's head and Dom didn't seem to mind at all. He had on the happy face that he got after they walked or went for a drive. "Did you have dogs?"

"All my life until I moved here. My last dog died a week before I fell and broke my hip. It's like he knew something was going to happen and didn't want me to worry about him. But I sure do miss Gideon." He absently stroked Dom's fur. "He was a Bernese Mountain dog. They don't live long lives, not like those yippy small dogs people carry around in their purse. I was lucky with Gideon, he survived fifteen years. Would have been sixteen that fall."

"That's a long time to be with a best friend." Angie reached out and touched Dom's face. "I hope I get twenty years out of this guy."

"You treat him right, you might."

"Angie, Angie Turner, are you back here?" A female voice called out from somewhere in the house.

"Sounds like you're being summoned." The grin made Randy's face look younger somehow. "And maybe you're in trouble. Carol doesn't like troublemakers."

Angie smiled and stood up, putting the chair back. "Then how are you still around?"

He chuckled and as they were leaving the room said, "You and Dom are always welcome to come visit me."

"Believe me, we'll be here so much, you'll get tired of seeing us." She paused at the doorway. Hadn't Carol said Randy was on his deathbed? The guy was old, sure, but he seemed to be coherent and alert. Maybe she'd been talking about the other resident.

"Miss Turner?" The woman called again, bringing Angie out of her thoughts.

"Coming." She was going to be spending more time with Randy. He loved dogs as much as she did.

Chapter 2

After they'd gotten a tour of the house and the crew had picked their three top projects, Angie and Felicia headed to the kitchen to get lunch started. Mrs. Stewart, or Carol, followed them. She pulled out a notebook from the bookshelf that held several recipe books.

"This is Randy's and Kendrick's dietary plan. There is a state dietician who comes quarterly to look at the food plan and make changes. She's been worried about Randy's weight lately, so she's backed off on some of the normal limitations. Mainly, she just wants him to eat. Kendrick is on a low-sugar diet due to his diabetes but other than that, you have free rein in planning meals." Carol handed the book to Angie. "Of course, if it's too much, I could just make them something separate from the main meal."

"We're chefs." Felicia took the book from Angie. "We're used to special requests for a dining room filled with people. Feeding this group is going to be a breeze."

"If you say so. I find it hard to find food they can eat and still taste good." Carol glanced out the door to where the guys were getting ladders out of the garage. "When it's busy, we eat a lot of oatmeal around here. Excuse me, I need to go help them find the third ladder."

Angie and Felicia shared a horrified look. Finally, Felicia glanced down at the notebook. "It doesn't say anything about using oatmeal as a replacement meal. The dietician says it can be used as a supplement if the residents are still hungry or find a meal not to their liking. She's using it to keep from cooking."

"Then we'll make up a batch of soups and casseroles to leave with her when we go. And I'll bring my testing extras out here a couple of times a month. My freezer is too full anyway." Angie took the notebook and closed it. "Let's get cooking. I think our residents might really need a good home-cooked meal."

Angie pulled out soup from the cooler that they'd brought for lunch the first day. "This Basque wedding soup should meet their dietary restrictions, right?"

"I think the only thing we're going to have to do is adjust the dessert recipes. We have fresh fruit I can make a salad out of for Kendrick. And we have brownies for the rest of the group. You get the soup warming up and I'll start making sandwiches." Felicia put her hair back into a ponytail and started working.

They were done just before one. Angie surveyed the trays they'd made for the residents and the rest of the food was set up buffet style for the others. "Should I ask if they want to come to the dining room and eat with us? According to Carol's notes, the residents eat in their rooms."

"That can't be fun." Felicia glanced around the room. "Hey, I'll go tell the others that food's ready and we can take the trays into the guys. Then we can sit with them for a while if they want us to."

"That's a good idea." Angie frowned as she looked at the lonely tray. "I'm going to put my soup on the tray too, that way I can sit and eat with Randy if he wants company."

"You're so smart." Felicia put a second bowl of soup on her tray as well. "I'll go sound the dinner bell and then take this in to Kendrick. See you after lunch."

Dom followed Angie to Randy's room. The older man was right where she'd left him, a book in his lap. She knocked on the door and he jerked awake. "I didn't mean to wake you, but I've got lunch."

"That smells wonderful. My late wife was a terrific cook. When I came home from being out of the country, I gained ten pounds in a month. Of course, we weren't eating too well that last few days before the city fell." He peered at the tray. "I may be hungry, but there's no way I can eat two bowls of that soup. I suspect you want to fatten me up while you're here."

"The second bowl is mine. I was wondering if you wanted company for lunch. I thought I might eat with you." She pulled a small table next to him and then set up the metal chair. As she did, Dom greeted the old man and then lay down next to his chair.

"I think your dog likes me."

"He's a good boy." Angie moved her soup closer toward her. "Eat before the soup gets cold."

"Now you do sound like my Mary Elizabeth." He smiled and picked up the spoon.

They were about halfway done with lunch when Carol came in, a tray in hand. "Oh, I didn't realize you'd already brought Randy his lunch. You don't have to do that."

"I wanted to. It's nice to share a meal with such wonderful company. Felicia's taken care of Kendrick's meal too." Angie set her spoon down near her bowl. "You should go eat. We'll handle this. You deserve a break."

"I usually give them their meds with meals." Carol wasn't giving up her status as head of the house easily.

"Did you forget the pills?" Angie studied the tray Carol held.

"What?"

"There's no bottles on the tray. Did you forget the pills?" Angie picked her spoon back up. "You can bring them in now if you want, but he doesn't need another food tray."

"Lord, no. I'm already stuffed." He scooped up the last of the soup with some of the bread from his sandwich. "But I'm still eating. Not to say bad things about your cooking Carol, but you really must try this soup. It's wonderful."

"My sous chef made it. It's his family recipe. We bring it out in the fall at the restaurant, but he always insists on making it himself. He won't tell anyone the recipe." Angie leaned closer. "I'm thinking he's using a premade soup base, but he swears it's all homemade. Well, as close as it can get in the restaurant."

"Well, I guess I'll come back with your pills." Carol turned and left the room.

He watched her go. "Carol's a nice lady but she really doesn't like people in her business. She wouldn't have asked for help if the state social worker hadn't told Carol if she didn't get the place up to code that the state was going to find other arrangements for Kendrick and me."

"I have to ask, how often does she feed you oatmeal for a meal other than breakfast?" Angie didn't look at Randy but she hoped he'd trust her with the truth.

"Now don't get that look on your face. Carol's doing the best she can. That's what we all do. Just the best we can." Randy covered a yawn.

"Do you want me to help you to your bed?" Angie set her empty bowl down and moved the table.

He shook his head. "I can make it. But there is one thing you can do for me."

"What?" Angie motioned to Dom to move out of the way. He came and sat by her feet, his head lolling on her thigh.

"Come back and talk to me later. I need a favor from you and I can't ask Carol. She gets a little testy around certain things." He shuffled to his bed, then turned around and sat. Carefully lifting his legs, he lay prone on the small mattress. "Just come back after my nap and I'll explain everything."

Angie carefully returned the chair, then grabbed the tray and motioned to Dom. He looked at Randy, then at her, then back to Randy. Angie slapped her leg and he moved toward the door. When they were out in the hallway, she reached down to pet his head. "I know you like your new friend, but he needs his sleep."

Dom glanced back at the room and whined low in his throat.

"What the heck?" Angie scratched behind his ears. "I've never known you to be this attached so soon."

"Attached to what?" Ian asked, coming down the hall. He'd taken ahold of the tray before he spoke, which was a good thing since Angie squeaked and about almost dropped it. "Whoa. You're freaked out about something. What's wrong?"

"Who. Dom's attached to and now nervous about his new friend." Angie handed Ian the tray and they turned to walk hand in hand to the kitchen, where they dropped off the tray, and then to the family room, where Carol was waiting for them. To face her wrath, Angie would need more than just a hoodie and a pair of running shoes.

"Thank you for lunch." Carol glared at Angie when she walked in. "I'm worried that your presence may upset the residents' schedule."

"I'm sure they could use some company." Ian sat on the couch and patted the seat for Angie to join him. "It must be hard being out here, isolated with just the three of you in the house."

"We have monthly visits from the social worker and a local nurse. And the dietician and doctor come quarterly," Carol sputtered.

"Yes, but that's paying people to talk to you. We're here on our own dime and spending time with your residents, just because it's the right thing to do." Ian nodded toward the group. "Maybe you should take advantage of our presence and take some 'me' time. We'll keep the place going."

Carol didn't quite know how to answer, at least judging from her facial expression. Angie had never seen a person that red before. *You got more than what you bargained for with this crew.* She wondered if Carol was just stubborn and stuck in her ways, or if something else was going on. "Hope, you and Bleak are on clean up kitchen duty. And if you're still there when I come back to start dinner, you can help me cook too."

"Sounds like a plan." Hope pulled Bleak onto her feet. The two girls paused, glancing at Carol, before they left the room. "Unless someone needs something else from us now."

"Nope, you're good." Felicia waved them away. "So glad we have the children along to do the dishes."

"I heard that. And I'm not a child," Hope called over her shoulder. A chuckle went around the room.

Angie sank back into the couch. "They grow up so fast. So what did you all get done this morning?"

"The walls are prepped outside and ready for a coat of paint, but I think we'll slow down outside and come in to do the room setup. I don't want to *need* to do this once a year." Estebe sat on the love seat, his big brawny arms curling around Felicia. "I think we may get more than three items off the to-do list."

"You could leave early if you get done before Sunday afternoon," Carol offered, a twinge of hope in her voice.

"Of course not! We'll just get more things done for you." Felicia seemed upset about the host's words, not for the first time. "There's nothing wrong with us staying around until Monday."

"Well, just remember if the residents start telling you about buried treasure or riding a motorcycle from San Diego to Seattle, it's a tall tale." Carol took two steps away from Matt, who'd snuck up behind her.

"Allowing them to tell us stories is the best medicine for a lonely heart. I intend to spend as much time as humanly possible with them. Besides, Dom loves Randy." Angie reached down and stroked his fur.

Carol pressed her lips together. "Well, just make sure you don't let him get overly tired. It's not good for him to go without his naps during the day."

Angie watched as the woman left the room, straightening a doily on the chair by the door as she walked by.

When the back door closed, Felicia shook her head. "That woman is wound as tightly as a grandfather clock."

"Are grandfather clocks on springs?" Matt asked Estebe. "I thought they had a pendulum system."

"That's not the point she's trying to make," Estebe responded.

Felicia sighed. "You know what I mean. The house isn't what I expected. Kendrick was scared to death to talk to me. Now, I know some men don't like talking to women, but he kept looking at the door, like he was afraid someone would overhear us and he'd be in trouble."

"I got the feeling Carol runs a tight ship, but I learned that she was forced to ask for help with the house by the state." Angie confided what Randy had told her. "Let's just keep our eyes out while we're here. It might be nothing."

Bleak stood at the doorway, shivering. "I overheard you talking. The place reminds me of home. We weren't allowed to talk to any strangers because you never knew who was with the state. We were told over and over that if the state came, they'd take us away from our parents and put us in an institution. With rats and gruel."

"Oh, sweetheart. I hope this isn't upsetting you." Ian stepped closer to the girl he now considered his cousin, even though she wasn't born into his family.

She lifted her chin. "As the great Gloria says, 'I will survive.'"

The room exploded with laughter and finally Angie stood. "Okay, we have our afternoon assignments. Keep your eyes open and work hard. This is for Randy and Kendrick, not for Carol. Just remember that."

As she and Bleak returned to the kitchen, Angie paused in the hallway. "Can we be serious for a minute? Are you okay?"

"I'm fine, really. When Felicia was talking about Kendrick, it struck a chord with me. I'm not saying it's the same as it is at the encampment where I lived, but it feels the same." Bleak narrowed her eyes and focused on a spot on the wall. "Does that even make any sense?"

Angie hugged her. "It does to me. And listening to your intuition is important. You see the world differently than the rest of us do. It's a good thing, believe me."

"Sometimes I wonder." Bleak turned into the kitchen and went back to the sink where Hope was washing dishes.

Bleak had grown up on a community farm in Utah. If Angie was being honest, probably in a cult. She'd handled her parents' household from a young age and was a hard worker. But when she'd been promised in marriage at sixteen, she'd run away to Idaho, where she'd wound up sleeping in the alley behind the County Seat. Ian had found her and taken her under his wing. Angie loved that about him. He was always looking out for others, no matter what the cost.

While Hope and Bleak were doing dishes, Angie started working on a shopping list for the center. She'd send Ian and Estebe to the store later this afternoon. She opened the pantry and started writing on her clipboard. The place needed everything. She leaned down and found pint jars filled with honey. The farm must have a beehive somewhere. Some of the jars still had honeycomb in them.

Smiling, she set the jars aside and kept working on the list. She found a trap door in the floor where potatoes, onions, and carrots were stored. She pulled out several and put them in one of the baskets stored nearby. A recipe for beef stew was forming in her head, if they had any meat to work with. She closed the root cellar door and looked around for a freezer.

Angie found it near the corner of the pantry. This room was huge and had plenty of shelf space. Carol just needed more food to put on the shelves.

When she opened the chest freezer, she found what looked like a side of beef all broken down to cookable pieces of meat. She found two packs of stew meat and pulled them out. Beef stew was what's for dinner. That and a nice cornbread to soak up the juices. She hadn't brought her cookbook, but this recipe she knew almost by heart. Besides, she had the ingredients on her phone as well since she and Felicia had been trying to finalize the recipes for the first annual County Seat cookbook.

She took the clipboard with the shopping list and the stew ingredients back into the kitchen. Hope was alone in the room drying the last few pans. "What did you find?"

"Actually, the freezer is well stocked. They need chicken but there's a lot of different cuts and types of meat and fish." Angie set the basket by the sink. "And there's a small root cellar to keep the vegetables fresh. Just not a lot of canned goods."

"Seems like the easy-to-cook and -serve items are always the first to go. Even at my parent's house." Hope eyed the ingredients Angie had brought out of the pantry. "There's a stock pot down here. I'll get it for you. I love stew."

Angie considered what she'd brought out as Hope found the pot. "I need another onion. And maybe there's some bones in the freezer for broth. Or even some packaged stuff. Right now I'm not picky."

She went back into the pantry and looked for the missing items. No bones and no broth. She'd have to make do. She dropped the onion she'd been carrying and ran over to get it. It had rolled into the pantry. She bent down and saw a box of rat poison on the floor under the food shelves. Angie picked it up by two fingers and took it into the kitchen. "Grab me a plastic shopping bag."

Hope got one and held it out. "Is this what you need?"

Angie slipped the box into the bag. Then she went to the sink to wash up. "I saw a shed out near the garden. Take that bag out there and tie up the top. Something like that should never be kept in a kitchen. I wonder why she wasn't cited for that before."

As Hope left out the back door, Angie started washing the potatoes. With such great produce around, she wondered how Carol didn't like to cook. Sometimes the quality of the ingredients made a huge difference in what came out of the kitchen. Of course, Ian ran the farmers market and didn't cook. When they'd met, he'd had what seemed to be a year's supply of canned spaghetti in his kitchen.

Chapter 3

With the stew slowly simmering in the kitchen and Hope and Bleak making cornbread, Angie had a few minutes to visit with Randy again. Dom hurried to the man's room and pushed open the door before she could open it.

"Well, hello little fella." Randy reached out to rub Dom's fur. "I'm so glad you could come back."

"Dinner's on the stove and I'm the only one without an assignment right now." Ian and Estebe had gone with Carol to find the local grocery store. Felicia had Matt and Nancy weeding the garden. "Did you have a nice nap?"

"The soup you made hit the spot. I haven't slept that deeply in months." Randy pointed to his end table. "Can you get the box out of that drawer for me?"

Angie walked over and got the box. Then she pulled the table closer and set the box on top where Randy could reach. She opened the metal chair and sat. "What's in the box?"

"Memories and regrets." Randy smiled at her, but he looked sad. "I need some help with a regret."

He took out a picture of a man and a woman and handed it to her. It was obviously their wedding day. The young man was in a dark suit and the woman in a modest wedding dress of white lace and satin, but the skirt ended at the knees. She wore a headdress with a puff of tulle on the back. They were both smiling.

"Beautiful couple. Who are they?" Angie set the photo back down on the table.

Randy picked the photo up again. "That's my son, Jacob, and the woman he married. Mai is her name. It's written on the back. The picture was in my wife's bible. I found it when she died."

"I don't understand. Didn't you know about the wedding?"

"Jacob brought her to meet us when he asked her to marry him. I was angry and stubborn. I told Jacob if he was going to marry one of *them*, he was disowned." He shook his head, tears in his eyes. "I spent years fighting the Vietnamese and he wants to marry this girl? Bring her into our family? I guess I was hurt that my time in the war didn't mean anything."

"But he married her anyway." Angie stated the obvious. "When did you last see him?"

"It's been over thirty years now." He set down the photo and looked out the window. "My wife, she kept in touch with them without letting me know. But I didn't even tell him when she died. I only had an old address I found later in her things. I should have told him his mother died. I guess when he didn't hear from her, he figured it out."

Angie let the words settle. This was Randy's story. He needed space to tell it.

"So now I'm an old man with a basketful of regrets at my feet. Can you help me fix this? Can you help me find my son?" Randy grabbed her hand and gently squeezed. "I'd ask Carol for help, but it's complicated. I need to know if he's alive. If he's happy."

"Of course." Angie pulled a piece of paper and a pen out of her pocket. "Tell me his name and where he lived the last time you knew. And his birthdate."

Randy gave her what he knew. Glancing at her watch, she saw she needed to get busy. "Sorry, dinner's coming up and I'm in charge tonight. I'll do some searching tonight and see what I can find."

"One favor. Please don't tell Carol. Like I said, she wouldn't understand. It's complicated." He stood and moved toward the bed. "I've got another nap to take before dinner. It's a tough job being this old."

Angie smiled and motioned to Dom to follow her. When she reached the kitchen he whined and stood at the back door.

"I'll get him," Bleak said as she opened the door. "I need a bit of a walk myself. Do I need the leash?"

"Please. And take a poop bag too." Angie washed her hands in the sink and laughed when Bleak wrinkled her nose. "Part of the fun of owning animals."

"I know." She grabbed the bag and tucked it in her shorts pocket, then clipped on Dom's leash. "Come on, big boy, let's go stretch our legs."

Hope pulled a pan of cornbread out of the oven. "She loves dogs. They weren't allowed to have pets at the compound. And she hasn't brought it up to the Browns yet."

"She only has one more year before she goes away to college. Can't really take a dog to the dorms." Angie cut a slice of the cornbread. She tasted it without butter or anything else. "Yum. This is really good. You guys did great."

"Thanks. I love making cornbread to go with stews and soups in the fall. My mom will bake bread some weekends, but I like the ease that cornbread has. Not so labor intensive." Hope cut a piece off and popped it into her mouth. "Bleak and I have been talking about renting a house in Boise maybe when she goes to school. She'll be working and I think renting will be cheaper than living on campus. And the thought of living in the dorms, well, it kind of scares her. Too many people."

Angie studied the young woman who'd started working for her as a dishwasher, the job Bleak took over when Hope moved to line chef. "Is that something you'd want?"

"I need to get out of the house. My folks are driving me crazy. Their house, their rules. You know the drill. And I like Bleak. We'd have fun together. I think Maggie's going to be upset if she doesn't try to rush a sorority, but she's just not into the normal college life." Hope looked around the kitchen. "How do you want to serve dinner?"

"Let's dish out bowls of stew and put them on a plate with two squares of cornbread. Then we'll put a generous pat of butter on the plate and more butter on the sideboard, just in case they want more. Do you think that will work?" Angie surveyed the room. "Then we can eat out on the deck or in the dining room."

"Are you eating with Randy again?" Hope pulled out bowls from the cabinet and set them near the stove and the stewpot.

"Actually, I think I'll ask Ian to sit with him. He might like to chat with a guy for a while rather than me." Angie looked out the back screen door and saw the van pull up. "Besides, I'm going to be busy putting away groceries."

Hope followed her gaze. "Cool, they're back. I'm starving."

"Let's get the stew dished out and then we'll eat. I'll put away the perishables and come sit with you and Bleak." Angie dished out the first bowl. "I'd like to hear more about this renting plan. Have you talked to Estebe? He might have a place for you that he'd let you rent."

"Great idea." Hope cut cornbread and set it on the plate, one square halfway on top of the other, resting on the plate. She put the butter on the left side of the bread and put a spoon and a butter knife on the plate. "How's this?"

"Perfect. And easy to pick up and move." She nodded to the two trays behind them. "Set up the trays with two meals and I'll send Ian and Estebe in to eat with Kendrick and Randy. I think we'll all take a turn with meal duties."

"Sounds good to me." Hope grinned as the men came into the kitchen, arms filled with grocery bags. "Welcome back. You're just in time for dinner."

"Good, because I'm starving." Ian sniffed the air. "Your beef stew. I'm in heaven."

"I'm glad you're in a good mood because you and Estebe are taking trays in to the residents. They need someone to talk to who has the Y chromosome." She pointed to the table near the inside wall. "Just set everything over there. I'll get it put away as soon as I eat."

Estebe held up a bag. "I'll put the items that need to be refrigerated over here to the left of the table."

"Perfect." Angie nodded to Carol as she came into the kitchen. Her oversized tote was over one shoulder and she carried one grocery bag. "I bet you're starving too, after having to deal with them at the store."

"They were fine. Perfect gentlemen." She noticed the filled bowls on the trays. "You're giving the residents way too much to eat. Their tiny stomachs can't eat two bowls full."

"Actually, the extra bowls are for Estebe and Ian. They're just getting the groceries inside, then they'll take their food along with them." Angie took the grocery bag from Carol and set it down on the table.

"I can't have you all just popping in on them all the time. They need their privacy," Carol protested.

"Men need other men to talk to," Estebe said as he picked up one of the trays. "It's the way of the world. We are here, we need each other's counsel."

Ian, Angie, and Carol watched as Estebe took the tray and headed toward Kendrick's room. Ian shrugged and picked up the other tray. "There are only a few more bags in the van. Can you send Hope and Bleak out to get them?"

"I'll get them." Bleak came into the house and let Dom off his leash. "I dropped his present, bag and all, into the outside trashcan. I figured you didn't want it in here."

"I'll help." Hope started to take off the plastic gloves she'd been wearing to set up the cornbread.

"Stay here and finish the dinner service. It won't take me more than two trips. I peeked in the back when I walked by." Bleak headed back outside.

Ian leaned over and gave Angie a quick kiss. "Talk with you later, okay?"

"Sounds good." Angie dished up another bowl of stew. "Are you ready to eat, Carol?"

Carol watched Ian until he disappeared into Randy's room. Finally, she sighed and turned back toward the counter. "I can't wait."

Hope handed her a completed plate and Carol left the kitchen and headed to the other side of the house. Angie assumed her living area was on that side. She dished up another bowl of stew. "How many more do we need?"

"Six," Hope said as she took the plate and put cornbread on it. "Five now. I get the feeling Carol's not too happy with having us here."

"She's not hiding her feelings very well." Angie dished up another bowl. "I wonder why she's so insistent on us staying away from Randy and Kendrick?"

"That is the question, isn't it?" Hope focused on setting the cornbread on the plate just right.

Angie finished dishing out the bowls, then texted Felicia that dinner was ready. "I'm sitting outside to eat. What about you?"

"Sounds great." Hope grabbed her plate and held the door open for Bleak to bring in the last of the bags.

"Except I forgot that I have to put away the perishables." Angie sighed and set down her plate. She went over to the table and started pulling out the items that needed refrigeration. Hope and Bleak picked them off the table and put them in the fridge. Angie cocked her head, studying the girls. "I thought you two were going to eat?"

"I will as soon as you sit down too. Many hands make light work." Hope smiled at her boss. "One of my mother's favorite sayings. Along with Jesus helps those who help themselves."

In just a few minutes, not only were the perishables put away, but so was all the food and even the paper products. Angie glanced around in pleasure. "Light work done."

The girls grabbed their dinners and headed outside to the deck. Felicia, Matt, and Nancy came in from the garden with their arms loaded with a pile of peppers and some late-season tomatoes. Felicia motioned for them to put the haul on the sink. "Look what we found."

"We'll meal-plan them into tomorrow's schedule." Angie pointed to the kitchen. "Come out and sit and eat with me. I've sent your fiancé off to eat with Kendrick."

"Sounds great. And I love it when you say fiancé. It sounds so French," Felicia said before heading into the kitchen.

Angie ate some of the stew. It was perfect. Of course, a different version would have had some red wine, which would have given the stew a different flavor profile.

She heard Felicia sit next to her. "I can't believe that garden. It's huge. But it looks abandoned. Like someone just stopped taking care of it."

"Carol doesn't seem like the gardening type. Maybe someone else used to live here." Angie leaned close and quietly told Felicia about her talk with Randy. "Can you help me do some research tonight?"

"Of course. We'll hide in our room and work on the secret project. This is turning out to be more and more like camp." Felicia tasted the cornbread. "This is so good, you don't even need the butter. Good job."

"Give the praise to Hope and Bleak. Those two are becoming quite good in the baking department." Angie polished off one of her squares. "You might not need to be the pastry chef soon."

"I like being the pastry chef." Felicia grinned. "It gives me permission to taste-test all the desserts. But it wouldn't be a bad idea to train a backup."

"Especially since you'll be gone for a month on your honeymoon next summer." Angie watched the sun starting to set in the western sky. One day down and she already had a mystery to solve. Maybe Ian was right. She might just be attracted to these investigations like a fly to honey.

"I can't believe I'm getting married next year. I always thought you would be first." Felicia leaned into Angie, hitting Angie's shoulder against her own. "Of course, I was praying Todd wouldn't ask you. He was just along for the gravy train. He never would have been committed."

"I don't disagree. Todd was a mistake from day one." Angie smiled at an old memory. One where Todd, Felicia, and she were tubing the Boise River. Todd had been fun. But when there was work to be done, he always had somewhere else to be. Kind of like a reverse Clark Kent and Superman.

"I don't think I've ever heard you say that and actually mean it." Felicia leaned back in her chair, looking up to the darkening sky. "It's such a lovely night. I'm so glad Hope set this retreat up. Of course, we need to sit down together maybe tomorrow and talk about the plans for County Seat's next year. I love thinking about all the possibilities."

"You make it sound like the restaurant's a living thing." Angie laughed as she finished her cornbread. "I do think we should do more volunteer activities like this and the time we served at the homeless shelter."

"I'm not sure I could get Estebe to agree to that. He's still a little miffed at the way Taylor treated our relationship." Felicia lifted up her left hand and stared at the engagement ring. Taylor and Felicia had been dating when the teambuilding outing had been at the homeless shelter Taylor ran. The relationship hadn't lasted long, especially after Felicia realized she was more arm candy for the center's fundraising events than girlfriend. "But maybe we could think about the food bank or the women's shelter."

"We could make our team outings a service project." Angie was getting excited about the options.

"Some of the time. The crew needs fun too," Felicia said.

Angie scoffed. "This isn't fun?"

"You were cooking all day. To you, cooking is fun. The rest of us were scraping paint and cleaning out the garden. Which still needs some work tomorrow," Felicia reminded her.

"Estebe said he wanted to be on the home projects, not cooking, but I guess I could switch out with Nancy or Matt." Angie had already been planning tomorrow's meals, but she could hand the kitchen over.

"Don't look like that. I'm giving you crap. Nancy wants to be on the garden crew this week and Matt, he's already started setting up the painting supplies to start tomorrow. The kitchen is yours. But you need to realize that the crew is really working hard."

"Angie knows this," Estebe said as he came out the kitchen door. "She is working hard to make delicious food for these war veterans. Kendrick said that the two meals she made was the best food he's had in years."

"That's the kind of compliment that keeps me cooking." She stood and picked up her plate. She reached for Felicia's plate. "Are you done?"

"Yes. The stew was lovely." Felicia glanced toward the kitchen. "Can I help you clean up?"

"I was hoping we could go for a walk down the road for a few minutes," Estebe said, glancing at Angie. "We haven't had a minute alone all day."

"You're such a romantic. Go ahead and take a walk. I've got a lot of people here who can help me wash dishes." Angie watched as Estebe held out his hand to help Felicia up out of the chair. They were a great couple and were going to build an amazing family. She moved into the kitchen and started working. Matt, Hope, and Bleak dropped their plates off and started out the door. "Where are you off to?"

"There's a pond down the road we want to check out. There's fishing poles in the garage and Randy says he used to catch trout in the pond." Matt grabbed a cookie off the plate on the counter. "I might just catch us enough for dinner tomorrow."

"Fishing's gross, but I'd love to see the pond. Maybe wade a bit in the water." Bleak moved around Matt and took two cookies, giving one to Hope.

Hope glanced at the dishes. She didn't follow the other two out of the house. "Do you need help with cleaning up from dinner?"

"No, you go ahead and have fun. I'll get these. Besides, Nancy and Ian are still around." Angie started stacking the plates and bowls.

"Actually, Nancy's in her room. She said she needed to call her kids and make sure they were following the rules for her mom, who's babysitting. I can stay and help." Hope glanced around, realizing that the pool of possible helpers for Angie was dwindling with each word out of her mouth.

"No, go ahead and have fun. I can do dishes." Angie waved a towel at Hope. "They're going to leave without you."

She shook her head. "No, they aren't. I was the one who talked to Randy about the pond. I popped into his room this afternoon to chat a little. He reminds me of my grandfather. He's in Oregon with my aunt, so I don't get to see him much. Anyway, Bleak and Matt don't know where it is so they have to wait for me. Thanks for cleaning up, Angie."

"We all have our jobs." Angie started the water and watched Hope glance around one more time, then she took off after her friends.

"I thought she'd never leave." Ian came in with the tray from Randy's room. "Randy's gone to bed and I'm reporting for kitchen duty."

"Are you sure you know the drill?" Angie took the plates from the tray.

He put the bowls by the others and then took a washcloth and soaked it in the soapy water. "I do. I was a professional dishwasher once. Well, for about a week, but nothing seems to have changed. Besides, we need to talk."

"Why, is something wrong with Randy?" Angie studied Ian's face as she put the silverware in the soapy water.

"No, but the pastor of Hope's church got a call from Carol about an hour ago. She told him that we weren't working out." Ian cleaned the other tray. "Angie, she wants us to leave the center."

Chapter 4

"What are you talking about? We're only scheduled here for three more days and the house isn't even painted yet." Angie dropped the plates into the sink and started washing them. "This doesn't make any sense."

"I know. And the pastor said we should stay here. He was just letting me know there's a bit of controversy going on. He talked her down. I guess he works with the social worker who's been assigned to the center from the state. If Carol doesn't let us help get this place up to code, she's going to lose her license and Randy and Kendrick will be moved to other places. Maybe that would be for the best, but I think something else is going on that Carol's afraid we'll find out."

"Why does she only have two residents?" Angie dropped her voice as she glanced around the kitchen. It wouldn't do for Carol to walk in on their conversation. "Do you know?"

"There were three, but one of the men died a month ago. The county sheriff called it old age, but the social worker was suspicious. She's asked for an autopsy, but since he's already been buried and had no relatives, she has to get a court order."

Angie thought about the rat poison in the pantry. She pushed the thought away. No one would be that cruel. "Carol wouldn't kill anyone. Would she?"

"We just need to keep together and keep her out of the kitchen while we're here. The social worker is working on finding out what really happened. If she's right, whatever killed this guy was slow acting. That's why the sheriff thinks it was his heart. The local doctor thinks he just went in his sleep." Ian put the plates he'd dried up in the cabinet. "I don't like gossip, but maybe she's onto something here."

"I just can't see a motive. This is her livelihood. She needs the residents to get paid for their care." Angie washed the last pot and after rinsing it, grabbed her own towel. "What was the man's name?"

"Phil O'Conner. I called Uncle Allen a few minutes ago and asked him to look into the place and any unexplained deaths." Ian stared down at the bowl he was drying when he added, "He says hi by the way."

"More like he said I can't believe she fell into another mystery. *What is with your girlfriend?* Something like that?" Angie knew Ian was telling a white lie because he had a tell. He didn't look at her when he lied. And he lied very badly. It just wasn't in his nature to be untruthful. "Anyway, I've got another project if you want to help me tonight."

"Finding Randy's son?" Ian finished drying the bowls. "Let's grab our laptops and a notebook and go outside with some hot chocolate. I think it's still light enough for a few hours for us to get a good start on it."

"He told you?" Angie ran the washcloth over the cabinets and stove. Tomorrow she was going to clean the oven as well as give the kitchen a deep clean. Even if Carol didn't want them there, she wouldn't be able to fault their work ethic.

"He did. He has a bit of a crush on you. I had to tell him you were my girl to get him to stop praising your kindness." Ian looked around the kitchen. "Everything washed and dried?"

"As far as I can tell. Let me grab Dom's bowl and some water and maybe he'll stay around the patio without being on a lead."

"Miracles do happen." Ian leaned over and kissed her. "Uncle Allen means well."

"I know. I'm probably touchy on the subject because he isn't wrong. I tend to fall into these things, but this one was so not my fault. Hope set up the team building. All I've done is pay the bills." She headed to her room to grab her notebook and her laptop. Dom followed her but then went past the room and sat in front of Randy's doorway. Angie went to get him and stared in at the elderly man. He was asleep in his bed, his hands over the cover and a smile on his lips. Angie grabbed Dom's collar and led him away from the room. She didn't want to wake him up, but she couldn't stop herself from wishing him good night. "Sweet dreams, Randy."

She gathered her stuff and found Ian already outside. Two cups of cocoa were sitting on the table, whipped cream on the top. "That was fast. I take it it's instant?"

"I'm not the chef." Ian grinned. "The whipped cream will help it taste better."

"As long as I didn't have to make it, I don't care." She filled Dom's water dish and then sat next to Ian. Dom positioned himself between the door to the house and them. She called his name and pointed out toward the garden and yard area. "The threats are going to be this way, buddy."

Dom glanced at her, then turned away and faced the door.

"He's not having the best retreat. He seems reserved. I've never seen him so quiet." Angie frowned as she watched her dog. "You don't think he's sick, do you?"

"No, he seems fine. Maybe a little subdued, but there are other people here. Maybe he's just overwhelmed." Ian reached down and scratched the top of Dom's head. "You okay, buddy?"

The question got a short bark in response, then Dom laid his head down again.

"Well, I guess we were told."

Ian looked at her, surprise in his eyes. "And what exactly do you think he told us?"

"That he's doing what he needs to do and to stop talking about him. It makes him crazy. He said you should know what he's thinking by now." Angie booted up her laptop and opened her search engine.

"You got all that from a bark?" Ian followed suit, watching her carefully.

Angie laughed. "You didn't? Seriously, you need to bone up on your dog translation skills. Bone up, get it?"

"It's not funny if you have to explain the joke." He leaned into his computer. "This is interesting."

"What did you find?"

"There's a Jacob Owens in Boise. Not sure if he's married or not, but it lists a phone number. He's a carpenter." Ian pulled out his phone and dialed a number. He grimaced and whispered, "Voice mail."

Angie listened to the generic message Ian left, and after he was finished she nodded to the notebook. "Write down the number and what you found. We'll may have to wait until tomorrow for a callback since that was probably his work number."

"I was hopeful." Ian picked up the pen and wrote a note.

Angie giggled. "Seriously, you thought you'd solve this mystery with five minutes on the internet and a phone call?"

"It could happen." Ian went back to searching. Angie found the next possibility and they went like that for the next hour.

They had ten names or variation of names on the list when they stopped. Angie closed her notebook and tapped the pen on the paper. "Maybe Randy and his wife lived other places when they were raising Jacob. He could have gone back to one of those areas. Randy was in the military."

"Military brats move around a lot." Ian nodded. "Good point. I'll write a note to ask Randy tomorrow."

"I'll take breakfast." Angie closed the notebook and set it on top of the closed laptop. Voices were coming up the road. Soon, out of the darkness, she could see Matt, Hope, and Bleak. Matt was carrying a fishing pole, but from what Angie could see, no fish. The girls were chatting a few steps behind. "Hey guys, want some hot chocolate?"

"Actually, I'm going to grab a shower and head to bed. I'm beat." Matt walked over to the shed and put the pole and fishing items inside. "No fish, but I got a few bites. Then my line kept getting snagged. Anyway, I'm going out again tomorrow night, just in case."

"Sounds fun." Angie turned to the girls. "What about you two? Hot chocolate?"

"Definitely, but we're making brownies too so we can make our own. You guys stay out here and relax." Hope shared a look with Bleak as they went inside, Matt following.

"Okay, so what was that look for?" Ian reached over and took Angie's hand in his.

Angie shook her head. "With those two? It could have been anything. Felicia said they've both been really involved in the wedding prep. I'm so glad she has someone to help her because if she depended on me, they would elope."

"You aren't a party planner. You never have been. That's Felicia's specialty." Ian nodded to the garden. "Do you think there's enough light to go for a short walk?"

"It's beautiful. Let's go." Angie picked up the leash and clicked it on Dom's collar and the three of them walked around the house and out to the country road. "Without road lights it's going to get dark quick out here."

"Sunset is an hour away. We'll walk for twenty, then turn back." Ian took Dom's lead and put his arm around Angie. "We'll be fine."

That night, Dom's barking woke Angie up in the middle of a nightmare. She couldn't remember what she'd been dreaming about, but the fear from the dream was still with her. She grabbed her phone and used its flashlight to find her slippers. Dom wasn't sleeping between her and Felicia. "Dom?" She called quietly

She shone the light on Felicia's bed. No Dom. She started to worry. She got up and searched the room using the small light. He wasn't on Nancy's bed either. Maybe he'd gone to find Ian in the middle of the night. He'd stopped barking. Or maybe she'd dreamed it.

She stepped into the hallway and saw him. He lay in front of Randy's room, blocking the doorway with his body. He lifted his head when he heard her approach and his tail gently thumped on the floor.

"Hey boy, what are you doing out here? Playing guard dog?" She reached down to rub his head and he licked her hand. Angie glanced into the room. Randy appeared still to be in bed, even though all she could see in the dim light of the nightlight in his bathroom was a man-sized lump under the covers. She shivered in the chilly hallway. Something had her dog freaked out about his new friend. Tomorrow she was going to call this social worker and see what she knew. She didn't feel right just packing up in three days and leaving Randy here. Especially if the last resident hadn't died of natural causes.

She went back into her room and lay there wide eyed, listening to the house sounds. Sometime during the night sleep had taken her back, and now Felicia was gently shaking her awake.

"Time to get up. I've made coffee and a batch of cinnamon rolls are in the oven." Felicia tsked as she studied Angie's face. "You don't look like you got any sleep last night. Maybe you should try for a few more hours."

Angie kicked the covers off. "No rest for the wicked. I'm grabbing a shower. Can you cut up some fruit to go with the cinnamon rolls? I'll make eggs for everyone as soon as I get dressed."

"Ian and Estebe ran into town." Felicia dropped her voice. "The social worker wanted to talk to them. Ian caught us up this morning. It's kind of chilling to be in a house where a murder might have taken place."

Angie took her friend by her shoulders. "It's worse when the murderer might be in the house with us. Just keep this to yourself, but make sure everyone stays in pairs. Buddy system and no one leaves the property without telling someone. Make sure the rest of the team knows as well."

"Hope's going to be devastated if this trip turns into a murder mystery too. She's still giving Matt grief about the fiasco at the penitentiary." Felicia took several deep breaths. "Okay, I'm okay. Everything's okay. It's going to be okay."

"New mantra?" Angie watched as Felicia visibly calmed down.

"New yoga teacher. She says situations are as much about how you approach them as the actual event. So now I'm going to assume the best out of everything and everyone. Then bad things won't happen." Felicia shrugged. "Or at least that's the hope."

"Stranger things have happened." Angie picked up her bathroom kit and clean clothes for the day. "I'll be quick."

"Just be careful." Felicia smoothed the comforter on her bed. "Nancy's in the kitchen drinking coffee. I'll go talk to her first."

"Don't worry anyone. Just let them know to be cautious." Angie didn't want her team freaking out. She ran into Dom in the hallway. He was standing by the doorway now, but when he saw Angie, he sat at attention. "Hey big guy. Can you wait a minute and I'll take you out after my shower?"

The squirm at the word out told Angie the answer was probably no. Matt came out of the other bedroom.

"Hey Angie. Does Dom need a walk?" He reached down and rubbed Dom's head.

"Would you please?" Angie held up her full hands. "I've got to get a shower still."

"No problem." Matt slapped his leg. "Come on big guy, let's go outside."

Dom followed Matt, but before he left the hallway, he turned back and looked at Randy's room. *Message received. You're still worried about him.* Angie glanced inside and Randy was sitting in his chair, reading.

She hurried to the bathroom, hoping that nothing would happen during her quick shower. If it did, her dog might not forgive her.

It took ten minutes but by the time Angie had finished getting ready, she walked by Randy's room and Ian was sitting with the man. Coffee cups were on the table. She caught his gaze and he waved at her. Hurrying, she dropped her stuff off on her bed and then went into the kitchen.

Everyone else in the house seemed to be there, except Carol, Kendrick, and Nancy. She stepped next to Felicia as she finished cutting up strawberries. "Is Nancy with Kendrick?"

"She just took him some coffee. They're talking about her kids. He has grandkids that age." Felicia smiled and then turned away from the others. "Carol's in the living room talking to the doctor."

"Why's a doctor here?" Angie tried to glance into the room, but she couldn't see anything.

"She said it's his monthly visit. I think she's trying to get him to say we're too much distraction for Randy and Kendrick." Felicia glanced around the room where Hope and Bleak sat talking with Estebe. "She really doesn't like us here."

"Well, I think she and the doctor need some coffee and cinnamon rolls." Angie dished up two of the rolls that Felicia had cooling on the stove. Then she poured three cups of coffee, and added a cream and sugar set and spoons. Picking up the tray, she nodded to Felicia. "Wish me luck."

She didn't pause at the doorway, just came right in the room and set the tray down on the table. Then she held her hand out to the doctor. "Good morning. I'm Angie Turner, owner of the County Seat over in River Vista. My kitchen crew is here working with Carol to get the home set up for new residents this fall."

"Nice to meet you. Carol was just telling me about you and your crew. I'm Ollie Norton. I'm the resident doctor for the area. I have an office over on the south side of Nampa." He took a whiff of the cinnamon rolls. "Carol, you must be in heaven having your own personal chef for a few days."

Carol mumbled something, but Angie didn't think it was agreement.

Angie turned her smile on Doctor Ollie. "Do you want a cinnamon roll? Tomorrow we're doing pumpkin donuts. Kind of a tribute to the season."

"I'd love one. And you brought out coffee. How nice." He beamed at her, then his grin dropped as he saw Carol's glare.

"I brought a cup for me as well." Angie set the rolls and coffees in front of Ollie and Carol and then the cream and sugar. She set the tray on the floor near her and sat in the wing chair next to the coffee.

"This is a private conversation," Carol said.

Angie nodded. "I know all about patient-doctor privilege, and I'll let you get back to that, but first I have some questions for the doctor."

"I'll try to answer, but Carol's right, my hands are tied on my patients." He dug his fork into the roll and took a bite. Angie could almost hear the groan he didn't let out. Felicia's cinnamon rolls were legendary.

"Okay, I was going to ask you about Randy. He seems a little depressed. I'd like to continue to visit after this week and I was wondering what you thought about me coming by with some baked goods. I noticed he doesn't have a lot of dietary limits." Angie sipped her coffee and watched Carol react to the news.

"I think that would be fabulous. Especially if you could get him to eat more. He's lost so much weight in the last few months. It's troubling." Ollie wiped his mouth with a napkin.

"You can't tell her that," Carol shrieked.

He stared at her. "Calm down, Carol. I can make statements that generalize my client's state. I didn't tell her how much weight he's lost or the percentages. I believe I'm the doctor here, correct?"

"Yes, Ollie." Carol went white. She picked up her coffee but ignored the cinnamon roll.

"That would be great. I'll put a visit on next month's schedule." Angie smiled at Carol. "This will be so fun. You won't know when I'm going to pop in."

Chapter 5

"Do you think one of us should go to the hospital to check on Kendrick?" Felicia and Angie were sitting in the kitchen at the center. Breakfast had been cooked and eaten. Dishes were washed and put away. The rest of the crew was in the garden or had started painting the outside of the house.

Angie shook her head. "No. It would look weird. Maybe we can take him flowers tomorrow. We have stuff to do here and only two more days to get it done."

"I can't believe how fast he got sick. Nancy said he was talking about his family and all of a sudden, it was like he'd had a seizure. I'm glad I wasn't in the room with him. I would have freaked out. Nancy was calm and collected. She stabilized Kendrick, called for Ian, and kept her cool during the whole thing." Felicia leaned back in her chair. "Okay, Angie, what's going on? You're too quiet and not feeding into or feeling my whole conspiracy theory."

"You haven't laid out a theory yet." Angie stood and got the pot to refill Felicia's coffee. "But I have to admit, he seemed fine yesterday. Can I tell you something else weird?"

"Of course." Felicia pulled in closer. "What do you know?"

"I don't know anything. I found Dom out in the hallway last night after everyone went to bed. You're going to think this is strange, but Dom appeared to be guarding Randy's room. And this morning, Randy's not sick like he says he's been, but Kendrick is. What if someone was going to give something to Randy, but Dom wouldn't let them?"

"That's probably pushing the limit for believability." Felicia looked around the kitchen. "Hey, where is Dom? Did someone take him out?"

Angie stood and motioned Felicia to follow. When they reached Randy's room, they saw Dom lying by the man's chair. Randy's hand was on Dom's fur and he seemed to be reading aloud to the dog.

Felicia started to say something, but Angie shook her head and pointed back to the kitchen. When they sat back down, she picked up her coffee cup. "The only times I've seen Dom act like that is when Ian's told him I was in danger and he had to watch out for me. I swear, Dom knows something bad has been happening to Randy and doesn't want it to happen again."

Felicia shrugged. "You could be right. Anyway, have you found Randy's son yet?"

Angie shook her head. "We have some calls out, but so far, nothing."

"Let me do some checking. I'll be right back with my laptop." Felicia stood and started to walk out toward the hallway.

"Bring my notebook too," Angie called after her. She studied the meal plan for the day. She needed to get some work done on the pantry as well. She wanted everything here to be as safe as possible. Even though she still didn't think Carol was doing this on purpose, she didn't want to take any chances.

As if she'd been pulled from Angie's nightmare, Carol appeared in the doorway.

"I don't know what game you're playing, but you need to realize I've been playing games a lot longer than you or any of your crew," Carol croaked.

"I'm not sure what you're talking about, but I wanted to get your take on an apple pie for dessert."

"You're not fooling me, missy." Carol came closer and Angie could see the crazy in her eyes. "You and your friends need to do your job and then get the heck out of here, never to return."

"Oh, but Doctor Ollie said…"

"I don't care what that old quack says. This is my house, my rules." Carol turned and left the kitchen. "I'm running to town on an errand. Please don't burn down the house while I'm gone."

"So apple pie?" Angie called after her as Felicia came back into the kitchen. Felicia set her computer down. "What was that about?"

"I think Miss Carol is getting tired of us being here. We know the social worker won't help her kick us out. Now she lost the doctor from her side. I wonder what she's trying to hide." Angie opened her notebook and started making notes.

"If the social worker has the power to get Carol to make changes, do you think she has a contract with the state for the home?" Felicia tapped her pen on the table. "We had to go through all kinds of licenses and such to open the restaurant. I wonder if it's the same for homes for the elderly."

"I saw a license in one of the cabinets. Hold on." Angie glanced around then went to the top cabinet over the stove. A folder filled with papers sat there. She pulled it down. "Go and see if Carol's car is still in the driveway. I'd hate to have her come back while we're snooping through her stuff."

Felicia went and stood at the living room window. "She's just leaving now. Well, she's in the car talking on her phone. Wait, she's pulling out and heading down the road towards Nampa."

"Watch for a few minutes and make sure she doesn't turn around." Angie grabbed the folder and took out her phone. She found a license that expired the next December. Felicia had been right. The home was certified. Next was a letter from the state about the deficiencies they found during an annual inspection. She snapped pictures of all the pages and of the license, then what must have been the original contract with the state. And there was another bunch of papers from the Veteran's Administration. Angie glanced through to find a contact name on that stack.

"She's gone. And I have Matt watching for her to return. What did you find?" Felicia said from her left.

"Lots of paper." Angie handed Felicia the stack from the VA. "Can you take pictures of that pile? Looks like I've got a lot of reading to do in the next day or so."

"How are you going to do that and help Randy find his son?" Felicia shook her head. "Let me and Estebe work on this in between our chores here. You and Ian focus on Randy's mystery. I'll figure out what's going on with Carol and the home. Divide and conquer."

"Sounds like a plan. I'll send you the stuff I take pictures of after we get this file gone through."

They worked for over ten minutes before everything had been photographed and copied into Felicia's phone. On the back of the file, she found a note. "There's a name and phone number on the folder. I'll take a picture of it too. Maybe it's another social worker."

Matt came into the kitchen from the back door. "She's coming down the road. Whatever you're doing, you need to be done."

Angie snapped the last picture, then they put all the papers back into the folder and put it away. Then she got out the flour and butter and a bowl. "Felicia, can you start peeling those apples?"

"Of course, but why?" Felicia went over and washed her hands. Then she lifted the colander full of apples out of the sink and put a grocery sack into the empty sink for the peels.

"I told her we were making apple pie. I want to at least look like I wasn't lying." Angie grinned at her friend. "Besides, once I get this done, I can start going through the cabinets and cleaning and restocking. Maybe there's something else of interest in there."

"I'll go out and work in the garden after I get these peeled and cut. Unless you need me for lunch?" Felicia was making short work of the apples.

Angie started mixing the pie dough. "No, we'll do soup and sandwiches again. I think I'm going to have the guys barbeque some hamburgers tonight and we'll do a couple of salads to go with it."

"There's a few melons out in the garden," Felicia added.

Angie floured the counter and then took the mixed dough out to finish mixing and rolling out for pie crust. "Go ahead and bring them in now. I'll cut some for a fruit salad for lunch. I'm really loving having the garden here and so many people to cook for."

"You do this every day at the County Seat." Felicia put the bowl full of sliced apples on the counter and poured lemon juice into the water to keep them from browning until Angie had time to finish the crust. "Well, every day we're open."

"No, we do short order stuff. One meal at a time. Cooking for a large group is different. They have to eat what I make." Angie rolled out the dough. "I want to spend some time with Randy today too."

Ian came into the room with the plates from Randy's breakfast. "I have a lead on his son."

"You do?" Angie's heartbeat sped up. Getting Randy and his kid together would be the best thing to come out of the trip to the veteran's home. At least someone would appreciate their involvement. Carol didn't even want them there. "What did you find out?"

"Actually, it's a hunch, not so much a lead. Randy said that Mai's folks ran a restaurant in Nampa when Jacob met her. There's still a Vietnamese restaurant open in the downtown area. It's been there a while, but I'm not sure it's the right one. How about we head out for a late lunch after you get the crew going? Maybe we can find someone to talk to who knows the couple."

Felicia was drying her hands. "I can handle serving lunch and cleanup."

"Sounds good. I'm assuming they don't open until eleven anyway. We can leave here as soon as I get lunch set up and we'll be back by three to start dinner. I'll make salads this morning." Angie frowned. She'd wanted to spend some time with Randy but this was a real lead, no matter what Ian thought.

"Can I help?" Ian glanced around the kitchen. "Or should I go paint for the rest of the morning?"

"Go help with the painting. We only have two more days after today and I want to get as much done as possible. I'm not sure Carol's going to let anyone else in to help." She glanced around the kitchen. "I'll start on one section of the shelving before I stop for lunch and salads. I should be done by tomorrow afternoon with the kitchen."

"With an attitude like that, Carol should be thankful we're even here. I can't believe how hard it's been to work with her." Felicia paused at the doorway. "Are you sure you'll be okay in here alone?"

"I'm fine. Besides, I have Dom." Angie glanced around the kitchen, looking for her dog. "Wait, where is he? Did someone take him outside again?"

Ian pointed toward the hallway. "He's right there."

Angie peered into the dark hallway. There in the middle of the walkway was Dom. He thumped his tail on the floor when he saw her looking at him.

"He's lying right past Randy's room. But he can also see you. I think even your dog knows there's something up here and wants to keep an eye out on you and Randy." Ian moved toward the back door to follow Felicia out. "I think you're safe."

Angie smiled at him. "I'm always safe. Just pop in now and then for a glass of water and make sure, okay?"

"I can do that." He paused at the door. "Just yell really loud if something goes down."

"Okay. Got it. Run fast and yell loud." Angie glanced at her notebook. "Maybe I should write that down."

"Fine, you can't fault me for caring." He paused before he went through the doorway. "Just stay safe."

"I will, I promise." Angie put the pie in the oven and started water to boil for the macaroni and eggs for the salads. She glanced up at the first section of cabinets and grabbed a step stool. "No time like the present, Nona always said."

She climbed up and opened the first cabinet. The bottom shelves were filled with dishes. The next row up had several polished wooden crates. She found a metal tag on one and brushed off the dust. Reading the name, she frowned. "Muffy?"

Checking the others, there were five in total, she realized they all had names on them. She read the name on the last box. "Rover."

She almost dropped the box when she realized what they were. Pet ashes. She took them out of the cabinet and set them on the counter. Then she went into the pantry and found a shelf way in the back with the larger cooking items. "Sorry guys, you don't belong in the kitchen."

Once that was done, she came back out of the pantry and caught Dom watching her. "Look, I'm not trying to be disrespectful, but they don't belong in the kitchen."

He laid his head on the floor between his paws and whined.

Angie wasn't sure if it was in agreement or fear she'd put him into a little box. Shaking her head, she focused on the job at hand. She washed her hands again, then went back up the steps to get the stuff off the top shelf. "This kitchen is getting scrubbed."

She took down several boxes. Opening one, she found a stack of letters. These were addressed to Mary Elizabeth Owens, Randy's late wife. Glancing around the kitchen, she opened one and read the first line. "Dear Mom…"

Chapter 6

"Why are we bringing this box with us?" Ian carried the box to the minivan.

Angie glanced around, hoping Carol was still eating and not watching them leave. "Keep it in front of you. I don't want her to see that we have it."

"Carol, you mean. You're stealing this from the house." Ian shook his head. "Uncle Allen is going to know I helped you so I guess I'll be in the next cell."

"It's not her property. Just get in the van and I'll explain." Angie climbed inside, then had Ian set the box on the seat between them. "I've been on edge since I realized what the box contains. They are letters from Randy's son to his mom. I bet she knew exactly where he was all along. This might just lead us to Jacob."

"Well, start reading. It's not a long drive to the restaurant." Ian started the van and pulled out of the driveway.

"I've got a plan. I'm going to read the newest ones first." She pulled her notebook and pen out of her tote. She quickly sorted the envelopes by postmark if she could read it. If she couldn't, she moved the envelope to the back, assuming it wasn't readable due to the age of the stamp. Then she started reading.

She'd gone through two letters before she found the first clue. "They live in Boise. Or did in 1995. She worked as a nurse at the hospital. He ran a construction crew. They built a house."

"Well, that might just give us what we need." He pulled onto the main highway. "I wish I had my computer. Does it say the name of the company?"

Angie studied the pictures that fell out of the envelope with the letter. School shots. A boy with dark hair and bright eyes grinned at the camera with a missing front tooth. The girl was shy, Angie could see it in her face, but the camera had caught a slight smile. "No, but maybe he told her before. They have two kids."

"Hold those out. Randy needs to see those." Ian smiled as she held up the pictures. "He's a grandfather and didn't even know it. I didn't know my grandfather and I wish I'd been able to meet him before he passed. Randy's meeting these kids. I'm going to make sure of that."

"He's only living in that home because he thought he was alone in the world." Angie scanned the next letter for clues.

Ian turned down the music. "That's not exactly true. He knew he had a son. He just couldn't get past his pride to tell him he was sorry before now."

"Even if it means you live in a room alone?" Angie shook her head. "I don't understand pride."

"Well, he took the first step, asking us to help. Now let's see if we can reunite this family."

The restaurant was in an area of downtown that hadn't been part of the renovation craze the town had gone through a few years back. The parking was on-street spots and Ian pulled into one close to the front door. Angie glanced at the old brick building that housed the restaurant and a pawn shop to the left. "Looks like we missed the lunch rush."

"I'm not sure they had a rush, today or any day since 1965." Ian exited the van and came around to open Angie's door. "You sure you want to eat here?"

"Some of the best places look like this." Angie smiled. "Just don't order anything raw. Or any seafood. We're too far away from the coast."

"Good hints." Ian took her arm and they walked into Jade Table. The décor was typical Chinese American restaurant in reds and golds. Asian was Asian back then, especially in small towns. The booths were covered with aging red leather and the tables were Formica. But the smell was heavenly. "My mouth is watering."

"Ginger, grilled veggies, sriracha, and lemongrass. I might have just found a new favorite." Angie glanced at the sign. "Where do you want to sit? The sign says to seat yourself."

"Over there near the front. That way I can watch the door." He put his hand on her back and led the way. "It's a habit I picked up from Uncle Allen. He always wants to see what's going on."

"He's a cop." Angie smiled at the young woman who came to greet them. She waited for her to drop off the menus and the water glasses. "I was wondering if you knew the owners of this place. They had a daughter named Mai. About twenty years ago, I guess."

"Sorry, my husband and I own the restaurant now. We kept the name to honor the former owners, but sometimes I wonder if we should have changed it. Business isn't great in this part of town." She leaned closer. "Wait! Are you Angie Turner from the County Seat? Ben and I love eating there."

"I am. I'm glad you enjoy it. Next time you're in, let me know and I'll bring you back to the chef table in the kitchen. You can see how we make the magic." Angie glanced at Ian.

"We'd love that." She held out her hand. "I'm Xandra Holmes. So why were you asking about the Nguyens? They're super nice people. They still live in the area. They have a house near Meridian."

"We're trying to find their daughter and son-in-law. His father lost touch with him years ago and now he wants to make amends." Ian took up the conversation.

Xandra pursed her lips thoughtfully. "I don't really know Mai. I think she lives in the valley. That's one of the reasons the Nguyens wanted to sell. They wanted to spend time with their grandchildren."

Ian pulled out a card. "If you would, could you call them and ask them to have Mai call me or Angie? I'll write both of our cells on the back. We'd appreciate it."

She took the card. "Okay, I can do that. So what are you thinking about for lunch?"

"Why don't you surprise us?" Angie held up the menu for her to take. "I'm excited to try your food."

Ian handed back his menu. "Can you bring us some hot tea as well?"

Xandra tucked the menu under her arm. "It won't be what you're used to getting in England. Oolong's softer."

"And I thought my accent had all but disappeared." He shrugged. "I'm not picky. I take my tea as it comes."

"We were just in London for a holiday. So my ear might be tuned to the accent." She laughed as the bell announced another customer. "You two have brought good luck. I never have much of a crowd after one. I'll get your food and tea right out."

As they waited for the tea to arrive, Ian pulled his notebook out of his jacket pocket. "Okay, so the Nguyens live near Meridian. I wonder if Uncle Allen could make some inquiries."

"It's worth a shot. I'm going to chat with Randy when we get back and see if he knows anything else about her family." She checked the tea. It was still not ready. "Do you think he'll want the letters? Why were they in the kitchen?"

"Maybe he asked Carol to move them out of his room. They could be a sore spot for him." Ian watched the new arrivals. It was a younger couple who were more interested in each other than the menus. He nodded toward the two in a booth near the back. "Young love."

Angie turned her head in time to see them curve into a kiss. "I don't think I was ever into PDA like that."

"I was. Especially when I was a teen. English girls are the best." He poured her a cup of tea. "Present company excepted and all that."

"Apology not accepted." She reached over and took his hand. "Thanks for playing Greg to my Daphne."

"All we're missing is our Scooby-Doo. Of course, Dom isn't really restaurant appropriate." He lifted her hand to his lips and kissed it. "Any time, I love investigating with you. Just don't tell Felicia. She thinks she and Estebe are Greg and Daphne."

"In her dreams." Angie met his gaze and remembered why she had fallen for Ian in the first place. His eyes, his smile, and yes, his accent all tied up in a very nice package.

"And here you are." Xandra set two empty plates in front of them, then started sitting other platters around the table. "I know, it's a lot, but Ben and I couldn't decide on what we wanted to show you. These are our favorites."

* * * *

After stuffing themselves at the restaurant, they headed back to the house. Angie curled into the seat and tried not to close her eyes. "I'm going to go talk to Randy first, then I'll start working on dinner for the team. What's your plan?"

"More painting. Estebe was going to start on the upper level as soon as he was done with lunch. I'm sure he'll need some help to finish off the front before the light disappears. We might be able to get all but the back done today." Ian turned off the highway and onto the country road that would take them to the veteran's home. "And I want to call the hospital and check on Kendrick."

"Good plan. We only have two more days here. We need to make sure it's safe to leave them here with Carol." Angie yawned, the sun coming through the window adding to the stuffed feeling she had from lunch making her crave a nap.

"There's nothing saying they aren't," Ian reminded her.

"Besides Dom. He scared someone away last night, I know it. And Randy was supposedly on his deathbed when we arrived, but he's actually stronger now. Then Kendrick winds up in the hospital." Angie shook her head. "There's something going on, we just don't know what. Yet."

"Old people have health issues," Ian reminded her. "But I agree, something's going on. Uncle Allen's looking into the last guy who lived here. Phil was healthy as a horse according to his girlfriend from the apartment complex—until he moved in here after breaking a hip. When he died, the girlfriend assumed she would get the life insurance, but apparently it went elsewhere. The agent wouldn't tell her when he changed the beneficiary or who it was."

"Can I have three guesses and the first two don't count? It's got to be Carol." Angie tapped her fingers on the dashboard. "Does Randy have an estate? Where is it going?"

Ian glanced over at her. "How would I know?"

"We need to ask him. And find out if he knows about Kendrick's estate," Angie nodded and whispered. "Follow the money. It's always about the money."

"If Carol had so much money, why wouldn't she fix the house?" Ian pulled into the driveway. "I think your Spidey sense is way off on this one."

"We'll see. Thanks for lunch." She leaned over and kissed him before they left the van. "See you soon."

"Yes, you will." He grinned and jumped out of the van. "But for the next few hours, I'm a master painter."

When she went into the house, she stopped at her room and tucked the box under her bed. Then she headed into the kitchen. Carol was there, standing in front of the cabinet that had a ton of fruits and vegetables that Felicia must have brought inside.

"Your garden's putting out some amazing produce." Angie picked up a cantaloupe and smelled the core. "This is ripe. I'm going to do melon cup for breakfast. You have quite the green thumb."

"Oh, my thumbs are black. My ex-fiancé was the one who planted the garden this year. He loved to work out there. I didn't get the attraction. I'd rather spend my free time reading. Look, I'm sorry I jumped at you earlier. I've just been so worried about Kendrick. I don't need to lose someone else." She closed her eyes but Angie had seen the pain in them. "Anyway, thanks for all you're doing."

"No problem. I did need to tell you that I moved the pet cemetery into the pantry. They didn't belong in the kitchen." Angie nodded toward the pantry door.

"Oh, my, I probably had forgotten I'd even put those there. They were Randy's pets. All five of them. He didn't like giving them up but he didn't have room for them. He hasn't talked about the ashes for years." Carol smiled. "Maybe he's learning you can't replace family and friendship totally with a dog. Even if they are amazing. Your dog seems to like spending time with Randy. He must know he's a dog person."

"They're very good at recognizing people who like animals." Angie glanced around the kitchen. Either the team had taken Dom out for a walk or if he was asleep somewhere. Angie figured she'd find him in Randy's room. "I was surprised you don't have a pet."

"I did, a long time ago. I had a cat. When he passed, I just couldn't bring myself to get another one." Carol smiled sadly. "Anyway, I need to be working on the paperwork. So many reports have to be filed, you wouldn't believe it."

"I'll come by when dinner's ready." Angie nodded to the apple pies sitting on the counter. "The pies turned out lovely."

"I can't wait." Carol hurried out of the kitchen and toward her office on the other side of the house. Her bedroom was that way as well.

Felicia came in the kitchen from the backyard with a colander of blackberries and with Dom. "There you are. How was lunch? Did you find our missing child?"

Angie leaned down to give Dom a hug, then answered Felicia. "Lunch was amazing. You have to try this place. And we didn't find him, but we have more leads."

"Well, it wasn't a total loss. Did I see you talking to Carol when I came up? What did the witch want now? Did she offer you a poison apple?" Felicia took the colander over to wash the berries in the sink.

"Actually, she was nice. And apologized for being horrible. So I guess we don't have to call her a witch anymore." Angie was looking at the vegetables and trying to come up with a recipe for dinner. "Her ex-fiancé planted the garden."

"Where did he go?"

"What?" Angie pulled her thoughts away from listing off the ingredients for a tomato pie and wondering if they had ricotta in the fridge.

"I knew you weren't listening. Her ex-fiancé? Where did he go?" Felicia repeated. "He had to be here in the spring to plant the garden."

Angie met her gaze. "She didn't say. And she didn't say why he left. I thought the 'ex' part kind of explained it."

"Unless he was the one hurting the residents." Felicia turned to face her. "We need to find out more about him."

Angie sighed. "Add one more item to the list of things we don't know."

Chapter 7

Angie knocked on Randy's door. She had a tray with tea and cookies in her hands. Dom stood at the door with her, waiting to be allowed inside. "Do you have some time to chat?"

"Let me see, my schedule is so busy. Of course, I have time. The question is do you? Carol says you all have a lot to get done in a short period of time." Randy reached out a hand and Dom walked over to see him. "It's been kind of quiet today without Kendrick around. He's usually in here talking my ear off about one thing or another. Although if he tells you he went to London during the war, that's a complete lie. He was kicked out of the Air Force just before the war started because of a heart condition. He showed them. They thought he wasn't strong enough to fight, but he's outlived a lot of boys that went over to 'Nam."

"I hope he comes back from the hospital before we leave." Angie pulled the table closer and poured the tea. "I didn't get a chance to talk with him. Did you hear what happened?"

"Reaction to a new medicine Doc Sawbones gave him. I think that guy uses us as guinea pigs for the new pharmaceuticals they sell him on. Carol said he's doing better and will be home tomorrow morning." Randy picked up a cookie and took a bite. "He sure loved meeting your friends. All of our visitors should be as lovely as your group is. And the girls. It's been a long time since I've heard girls giggling late at night. My sisters used to do that when we went to bed. They're all gone now."

"I hope we're not disturbing your rest. I could talk to them." Angie watched as Randy poured sugar into his tea. A lot of sugar.

"Doesn't bother me. I like waking up to that sound a whole lot better than when Carol had her man living with us. I didn't like the way he talked to her. And he looked at us like we were paychecks rather than people. I felt like I was that orphan boy in Oliver Twist." He laughed as he picked up the cup. "And I'm feeling a whole lot better now that he's gone. Now, I'm not saying he was messing with my food, but my stomach is much better now. You can make your own conclusions."

Angie thought of the rat poison she'd found in the pantry and shuddered, hoping her reaction didn't show. She didn't want to scare Randy. "So why did he leave?"

"Carol got smart and kicked him out. He wasn't a good man." He glanced at the door and lowered his voice. "She could do so much better. I think he was just here for a place to stay, but I'd never say that to her face. She works so hard."

"You like her." Angie tried to hide her surprise.

He blushed and tucked his head down. "Now, don't you go spreading rumors. There's no fool like an old fool, right. Anyway, Carol's going to be fine. At least she will be when I pass. I don't have much, my savings and a life insurance. Of course, if you find Jacob, I'll need to change that."

"Did you know they had kids?" Angie pulled out the pictures she'd had tucked in her jacket pocket. "He and Mai had at least two. A boy and a girl. Their names are on the back of the picture."

He studied the photos, turning them over and then back, a small smile on his lips. "The boy looks just like Jacob did at that age. Where did you find these?"

"There was a box with your late wife's letters in the kitchen. I suspect you must have brought them with you when you moved in." Along with the pet coffins, she added silently. "I take it you didn't look at the letters?"

Randy shook his head. "When Mary Elizabeth died, I fell into grief. I stayed there for years. Some people from the church came and boxed the house up when I sold it and I moved in here. They must have realized they were sentimental."

"There are several from Jacob to his mom. Maybe twenty. Do you want them? I have them in my room." Angie realized she couldn't say it was because she'd thought Carol might toss them, so instead she said, "I wanted to have time to study them for clues."

He looked up from the pictures he now held with a death grip. "Did you find anything?"

"Mai's folks ran a restaurant in Nampa, like you told Ian. We went there today for a late lunch." She didn't want to get him too excited, but she could see the interest dance in his eyes. "They'd sold the place to a really nice couple. She said she'd give the Nguyens my phone number and ask them to call me. I told her I was trying to reach Jacob. She said the in-laws lived in Meridian."

"I remember them. Mary Elizabeth dragged me to an engagement party they held at the restaurant. They were nice people, but I was so mad. I was rude to them." He reached down and petted Dom's head. "I really need to talk to Jacob. Do you think you'll find him before you leave?"

"If I don't, I'm not going to stop trying." Angie patted his hand. "You'll see Jacob again. Sooner than later, I hope."

He yawned and Angie took that as a clue to leave him alone. "Sorry, I'm just so tired all the time. I never slept through the night when I got back in country. Not for years. Mary Elizabeth used to try to get me to take sleeping pills, the ones you can buy over the counter. But I hate taking any pills. I only do it here so Carol doesn't get all up in my face about it."

"I'll bring the letters in as soon as I finish reading the last few for clues. Unless you don't want me to." She paused at the door. Dom had already laid down, blocking the doorway to get into the room. She might have just lost him to Randy. He obviously wanted to protect the older man.

"I'd love to see them. She used to write me when I was in Vietnam too. I'd love to catch up on my son's life." He lay down and pulled a cover over himself.

Dom looked at her and whined.

"It's okay buddy, you can stay here. Just come get me if you need to go out, okay?" Angie could swear that Dom knew exactly what she'd said as he laid his head down and closed his eyes.

Felicia was in the bedroom reading the letters when Angie came in. She didn't look up but spoke. "Hope and Bleak are getting dinner ready. These letters are so sweet. I don't think I've gotten a letter from anyone for years. Emails, yes, but not a real handwritten letter."

Angie sat on her bed and pulled out the last few envelopes she hadn't opened yet. "Look for anything that nails down where they live or work. We need to find Jacob. Randy is counting on us. He made Carol his heir before he decided to find Jacob. Those kids need a grandfather."

"Wow. That's a motive to actually get rid of him." She paused, setting down the letter. "Ian found a bottle of eye drops in Kendrick's room. The hospital is checking his blood work to see if he's been poisoned."

"I thought it was his heart. Randy thinks it's a reaction to a new medicine." Angie thought about how Dom hadn't wanted to let anyone in Randy's room. Had he scared away whomever had the eye drops and they'd gone to Kendrick's room instead? "I wonder who's named in Kendrick's will."

"Do you think she keeps the residents' wills on site?" Felicia whispered, glancing around the room.

"Where is Carol right now?" Angie glanced at her watch. Almost four. If the woman had planned to visit Kendrick, she would have to leave soon.

"In her office. Do you want to go offer her the last slice of apple pie? She seemed to enjoy it last night." Felicia curled up on the bed. "I need to get up to speed on these."

"I'll be right back. Dom's in Randy's room. Take him out if he asks, okay?" Angie stood and set the letters down gingerly on her bed.

"Dom knows I'm his employee." Felicia nodded toward the door. "Go get going. Maybe we can figure this out tonight and not have to sleep under the same roof as a killer."

"As an alleged killer." Angie smiled and headed out to the kitchen. She waved at Hope and Bleak as she made her way through the kitchen and to the hallway where Carol had her private quarters. An office, a bedroom, and a bath, all off a hallway with a sign on the wall with one word: *Private.*

She knocked on the door to the office; no answer. She poked her head in, but she didn't see anyone, just a pile of papers on the small desk. And all the chairs, except one, had piles of papers. Angie stepped inside and saw a real estate poster, a business card stapled to it. She read it aloud. "Let me know when you're ready to sell. I've got a ton of clients who would love this property."

She's selling? Angie peeked on the back of the card. Theresa Yard's name and smiling face was on the front. Angie studied the room. If she was going to actually search for something, she needed some time with Carol out of the house.

Shutting the door quietly, she moved back to the living room, where she peeked out the front windows. Carol's car wasn't in the driveway. She moved to the kitchen and leaned on the wall in the arched walk-through. "Hey, have either of you seen Carol?"

"She ran into town," Hope said, stirring a pot on the stove. "She wanted to visit the hospital. You just missed her."

Okay then, that was a great sign. The lords of chance were telling her she had an open window to do a quick search. Angie nodded. "Bleak, could you watch out the living room window and tell me if she's coming back before I get done what I need to do?"

Hope shook her head. "You shouldn't be sneaking into Carol's private area. It's not right."

"I know, but I found a flyer saying she might be looking at selling this place, and if she is I don't want our 'charity' work to be used for someone else's gain." Angie also wanted to find out if Kendrick's will listed Miss Carol as the beneficiary, but no need to mention that.

"Well, I guess that's a good reason." Hope frowned. "I bet that was a survey post we found down by the pond."

"The one that Matt got his fishing line wrapped around?" Bleak grinned at Angie. "Twice."

"Yeah. I knew that looked familiar. When my folks sold my grandfather's farm, they had to have it surveyed before they put it up for sale as the lines with the neighbor were in dispute. Has Mrs. Stewart just been using us to get the house ready to sell? Where would Randy and Kendrick go?" Fire spit through Hope's eyes as she thought about the two elderly residents. "That's not right."

"No, it's not. Anyway, Bleak, can you be my lookout?" Angie hoped the girl would agree the transgression was worth the sin.

"Sure." She grinned at Angie. "I haven't done anything like this since I moved in with River Vista's police chief and Maggie. I swear that guy knows what I'm going to say before I even think it. Especially if I'm trying to hide something."

"Like kissing Ty after prom?" Hope teased.

"La-la-la, I can't hear you." Bleak ran to the living room couch, where she planted herself backwards to watch the driveway. "Angie, you better get busy. I don't think she trusts us enough to leave us alone in the house for long."

As well she shouldn't. Angie made her way back to the office and started going through stacks. Medical records, bills, household lists, emails Carol had printed off. The stacks were all about running the home and the warnings she'd gotten from the state on fixing the place up. The pile on the chair was about the last resident, Phil, whom Randy had mentioned. The one who'd died in the house. And a notebook sat on the pile. Dates and meals and a note about some guy named Brett's whereabouts on each day.

Was Brett the ex-fiancé? And had Carol been trying to prove his guilt? Or his innocence? She pulled out her phone and took pictures of the notebook entries. Then she went to the file cabinet. If there were wills in this sea of paper, she'd have them put away, somewhere. Especially if she planned on cashing in after the guy's death.

Luckily, the file was in the top drawer. Carol had three files in the will section and a stack of blank wills also in the drop file.

Angie glanced through each will and found the listed heir. In each case, it was Carol. And the wills were all dated within the last few years. Angie leaned on the desk, breathing hard. What exactly had Hope brought them to? Was Carol some sort of medical black widow? Not marrying the men, but taking care of them for the sole purpose of inheriting whatever riches they had at the end?

And worse, was she hurrying things along? Angie needed to talk to Ian's uncle, Allen Brown. He was the River Vista police chief and he could tell her if she was just seeing unicorns when there were really only horses.

She snapped pictures of the three wills, then put them back and looked around the room. She thought it looked like she hadn't been there. She turned around and ran straight into a man who'd been watching her.

"Oh, excuse me." She tried to walk around him. but he moved in front of her. "I'm expected in the kitchen."

"Actually, everyone's outside putting out a fire near the garden. You and your dog are cramping my style. Maybe you should get in your vans and leave tonight like Carol suggested." He leaned close and touched her hair. "You smell like lavender. I do love a fresh floral on my girls."

"One problem with that. I'm not your girl." Angie knew who was standing in front of her. The framed picture of Brett had been in Carol's trash. She could see Dom coming up behind the man, his teeth bared. She decided to push her luck and guess at a few things. "My dog doesn't like you at all. You should leave now, Brett. Carol threw you out once. She shouldn't have to do it again."

"Leave Carol to me. There's no way I'm letting her get all that money when the next two guys croak. Besides, the girl's in love with me." His eyes hardened. "Most girls want me."

Dom growled behind him.

"One last chance, leave now. Or Dom will chase you out," Angie warned. Dom was over one hundred fifty pounds, or had been at his last vet checkup. She thought he could hold his own with Brett as long as the guy didn't have a gun or a knife on him.

He held up his hands and moved toward the side of the hallway. Dom watched and moved with him until the dog was standing in front of Angie, and Brett had a clear path to the doorway. Or it would have been a clear path. Now Carol stood there, a bag in her hands and anger on her face.

"I thought I told you never to come back." Carol advanced toward Brett. "You get your sorry butt out of my house."

"Our house. And our realtor wants to put it on the market. She has a buyer, sight unseen. And it's a good price. You just need to get the last two old coots out of here. I've been trying to help." Brett's tone changed and Angie could see why women fell for him. He had a silver tongue built for lying.

"You hurt Kendrick, didn't you?" Carol shook her head. "I didn't want to believe it. But you hurt Kendrick and you killed Phil. Just for money."

"Not just for money, for you. For us." He stared at her, then at Angie. "Now look what you did. We have a loose thread we need to snip off. Kendrick wasn't supposed to be the one in the hospital. Randy was my target, but the dog wouldn't let me in the room." He started toward Angie, and Dom stood, baring his teeth.

"Brett, stop. Leave her alone. And just leave. I won't call the cops if you go now and never come back." Carol's eyes brimmed with tears. "Please get out of my life."

"Actually, you don't have to call the cops, I've already done that for you and they're here." Ian stood behind Carol. He placed his hands on her shoulders, then moved her behind him as officers ran in with guns drawn and surrounded Brett.

Once they had him handcuffed, Dom let out a bark and turned to give Angie a sloppy kiss.

"I'm all right. Thanks for the assist there." She knelt and gave him a hug. "You're awesome."

"Stupid dog," Brett muttered.

Police Chief Allen Brown stared at him. "You have the right to remain silent. I suggest you follow that instruction. Brandon, read him his rights. Angie, are you all right?"

"I'm fine, but I'm confused. Why are you here?"

Bleak came around Ian. "I called him as soon as I saw that guy set the fire. Everyone ran outside to put it out and I knew something was going on. I had Allen on the phone when he came into the house through the side door. I put Allen on speaker phone and got as close to you as possible without being seen. After calling Dom to help, of course."

"Lucky I was out in the county doing a drive around today or it would have taken me twice as long to get here from the station." Chief Brown hugged Bleak. "You did right by calling me. Even if you weren't quite sure what was going on. You have good instincts. Maybe you should go into police work rather than hospitality when you go to college."

"You're just saying that to be nice." Bleak blushed but had a huge smile on her face.

Angie grinned at the newest member of the County Seat family. She had followed Angie's instructions, but broken them when she saw danger. And she'd improvised. "I'm proud of you. Thanks for saving me."

"I wouldn't have allowed him to hurt you," Carol said from the side of the hallway. "I'm tired of people getting hurt. Chief Brown? I think I have the evidence to allow you to convict Brett for murder. Along with several other crimes."

"I did it all for you. For us," Brett screamed as the officers dragged him out of the house. "We were supposed to be together forever."

"That would have been a very long time." Ian came to Angie and took her in his arms. "I'm glad Dom took care of my light work."

Angie laughed and relaxed into his arms. "I can't believe he thought he could get away with killing whoever he wanted. I'm sorry I was snooping, Carol, but I wanted to see if Kendrick had made you his heir."

Carol nodded. "He did. And so did Randy. I guess I thought I was helping, giving them a person to take care of. I should have realized that Brett was poisoning them."

"Do you mind coming into the station with us? I've got some questions that need clearing up." Ian's Uncle Allen took Carol's arm and started leading her out of the hallway.

"Wait, we need the proof." Carol picked up a tote bag that was sitting on a chair. Then she tucked all the papers and the notebook into the bag. She stopped and looked at Angie. "Will you stay with Randy until I get back?"

"He won't be left alone, I promise." Angie met Carol's gaze and the woman nodded.

She smiled. "I believe you."

Then Carol walked out of the house at Allen's side. The County Seat crew filed into the hallway.

"Let's go into the living room and sit. I'll tell you all about what happened there." Angie led the way and then explained the last few minutes to the people who meant the most to her. Her work family.

Chapter 8

The next morning, Angie made a special breakfast. Bacon, made-to-order omelets, muffins, hash browns, fruit bowls, and mimosas. The front door opened just as she was finishing with the fixings for the omelets.

"I'm here with the package," Ian called out.

Angie wiped her hands on a towel and went out to the living room.

Jacob and Mai Owens stood there looking around with not two but three children. Randy was going to be surprised. Angie stepped over and held out her hand. "Mr. Owens, I'm Angie Turner. Are you ready to talk to your father?"

He shook her hand, covering hers with his other hand. "We've been trying to make contact since Mom died. First, he wouldn't talk to anyone. Then he just disappeared. I've been so worried. I thought maybe he was drinking his pain away."

"No, he was here." Angie smiled at the woman, who was too pretty and had all three children cuddled next to her. They were all touching her. Her hand, her arm, her shoulder. The kids were scared. "Let's go talk to him and then I'll bring in your breakfast trays. Any requests for omelets?"

"Denver, please," the young girl called out and her mother smiled down at her.

"Denver will work for all of us. Thank you for making our breakfast. It's not often a chef of your caliber cooks for a family event." Mai put her hands on the kids and met her husband's gaze. "I'm ready when you are."

"Then let's go talk to Dad." He straightened his shoulders and girded his loins against the fight he thought was coming. Instead, he was going to be met with love and attention, something he'd probably thought his dad would never give him.

Angie loved it when people outshone others' expectations of them and were even cooler. Randy's son and family could have refused to be part of the old man's life after the pain he'd caused, but they'd been open to at least starting a dialogue. Angie hung back and let the group go inside the room. Dom was in there with Randy but when Jacob and Mai went in, Angie called him out.

"This is a family reunion, big guy." She patted his side and he followed her as she went back into the kitchen to cook.

As she finished fixing the details of breakfast, Angie pulled out the list of things that needed to be done. Carol needed to get new residents into the building now that she was probably losing Randy. And before that could happen, she needed to be cleared of the legal issues and the house needed fixing. She read out the next items on the lists. "We have one more day here. What are we going to do now?"

* * * *

After breakfast, Angie waited for the family to leave before going into Randy's room. He was sitting at the window, watching the world pass by, but Angie could see a weight had been lifted off the older man's shoulders. "Okay if I pull out these dirty dishes?"

"You do what you need to do. Don't mind an old man reminiscing." Randy greeted Dom as if he hadn't seen him forever. "I hear you were a brave boy yesterday."

Dom slapped his tail on the floor several times. Then he wandered the room.

"He was amazing. How did your visit go?"

He shook his head and Angie's heart sank. Maybe Jacob had told him it was too late to try?

"They have a mother-in-law suite that they are moving me into next week. I'm going to live with them. Even with all the trouble I caused, they forgave me." He blinked away tears. "But you didn't tell me how you found them."

"Ian got a call from the other grandfather. He told us where to find Jacob and Mai. He said it was only right to honor the elderly." She thought of the words that Ian had repeated to her, mostly because he'd not believed it himself. "Be good with the kids. I hate to see you back in one of these after being hardheaded about something else. Like the proper way to fry a chicken."

"Don't worry. I'll be on my best behavior. And when I'm not, I'll try. That's all I can do, right?"

She leaned over and kissed him on the cheek. "I'm so happy for you." As she left the room, Ian took the stacked trays. "You did a good thing here." "Your uncle would say I was meddling again."

He laughed and nodded. "I can't argue that. But you did a great job. I was busy finding the clues to put a family together and you were trying to convince everyone that someone had been murdered. Never an easy feat."

"Maybe not easy, but easier with you and my County Seat crew." She motioned toward the counter by the sink. "Set those down and I'll finish washing dishes. Then we need to run into town and buy enough food to fill these cupboards."

As Angie washed dishes she thought about the last few days. Another solid case solved by the Scooby-Doo crew. She loved her friends and family. And that was the way it should be.

About the Author

Photo by Angela Brewer Armstrong at Todd Studios

New York Times and *USA Today* best-selling author Lynn Cahoon writes the Tourist Trap, Kitchen Witch, Cat Latimer, Farm-to-Fork, and Tuesday Night Survivors' Book Club mystery series. No matter where the mystery is set, readers can expect a fun ride.

Sign up for her newsletter at <u>www.lynncahoon.com</u>.

Printed in the United States
by Baker & Taylor Publisher Services